White Elephant

Trish Harnetiaux

Simon & Schuster

NEW YORK   LONDON   TORONTO
SYDNEY   NEW DELHI

Simon & Schuster
1230 Avenue of the Americas
New York, NY 10020

First Simon & Schuster hardcover edition October 2019

SIMON & SCHUSTER and colophon are registered trademarks
of Simon & Schuster, Inc.

For information about special discounts for bulk purchases,
please contact Simon & Schuster Special Sales at 1-866-506-1949
or business@simonandschuster.com.

The Simon & Schuster Speakers Bureau can bring authors to your
live event. For more information or to book an event, contact the
Simon & Schuster Speakers Bureau at 1-866-248-3049
or visit our website at www.simonspeakers.com.

Interior design by Paul Dippolito

Manufactured in the United States of America

1   3   5   7   9   10   8   6   4   2

Library of Congress Cataloging-in-Publication Data has been applied for.

ISBN 978-1-5011-9990-5
ISBN 978-1-5011-9992-9 (ebook)

White Elephant

PART ONE

The Preparations for the Party

As I write this, I sit at the small desk in the living room.

It's just after 9 a.m., not a cloud in the sky, 74 degrees. I've always preferred Aspen in the early summer. A paradise.

I need to tell you something important before I go. Before I die. It's difficult to write that word. In these last couple weeks since the scan and diagnosis I have tried to accept it. It is impossible. I will miss you too much. I don't worry for myself. I am not afraid of death. I have lived afraid for too long. I will not die afraid. And I will not waste the time I have left.

It's important to tell you everything. I should have done it a long time ago. I'm sorry. I'm sorry you will have to carry this with you like I have. But you deserve to know before there's no one left to tell you the truth.

Claudine

By midnight the snowfall would reach a foot, just shy of breaking Aspen's one-day record set more than forty years before. No one predicted the storm would be so severe. The sheer speed of it. The first flakes didn't even start coming down until around two that afternoon.

Claudine couldn't see them outside the salon's picture window, her head stuck under a hooded dryer. With a freshly French-manicured hand, she reached into her cream-colored Chanel flap bag and pulled out the guest list: not counting herself, Henry, and their six employees. There hadn't been much time to put the list together. Zara had let her know she was coming just a few days before. Considering the short notice and how packed Aspen social calendars were during the holiday season, these were good, solid choices:

Captain and Mrs. Tiggleman
Kevin and Jerry
The Alpine Brothers

Old-school residents with character and charm. And, of course, purpose. The Tigglemans could rave about both houses she'd sold them—and show Zara that Aspen, unlike Hollywood, didn't favor youth but was a place where one could age with class and grace. Henry's childhood friend Kevin and his husband, Jerry, would demonstrate their long-standing connection to the town—and its inclusive, liberal side. And the Alpine Brothers, Jack and Bobby, with their ability to talk for hours about how to curve wood just right or the best temperature to melt steel, would indicate the firm's expertise, their insistence on working with only the finest contractors.

Claudine could have gone wider with the invitations, but it would have been a mistake to think packing the party with a room full of insipid millionaires was the right move to impress a pop star. The start-up bros who'd been invading town for the past decade brought a unique sense of soullessness and poor taste—the latter slowly destroying the business of Calhoun + Calhoun. Tech geeks who'd spent their entire lives wanting to blend in had no appreciation for Henry's artistry, the singular vision he brought to every architectural project. He put his heart into each of his houses—or at least *had* put it into them, until the health scare a few weeks ago. No, the new-money crowd only wanted acceptance and would rather buy a prefab cookie-cutter monstrosity like Steve Gilman specialized in rather than let Claudine sell them a true masterpiece.

She tried not to think about Steve. Though that was hard. These days Aspen was crawling with real estate agents like him. No discretion or discernment. Quick to sell whatever clapboard mansion came available. To think, the two of them were once the only upscale agents in town. (And once briefly—though not briefly enough—more than that.) Now there were dozens. The recession had driven a lot of brokers working mid-tier price points into their section of the market, and things continued to get more crowded thanks to the internet—Zillow, Trulia, Redfin. The only way to survive in this business was to sell big.

And Calhoun + Calhoun was just barely surviving. How bleak had things gotten? Well, just look at this salon. For years Claudine had been going to Lather—was one of Jeff's very first clients. He was the only person she trusted to get the sharp jut of her black bob just right. An overly severe angle looked like she was trying too hard to be hip, desperate to seem younger than fifty-three. Not angled enough, and she seemed too matronly, looked ten years older. There was a precision to it, but precision is expensive. Which now she couldn't afford. She had to come to a dump like this where instead of the soothing strings of Beethoven they pumped in too-loud Top 40 hits, and rather than glossy, oversized European fashion magazines the reading material was cheap, well-thumbed supermarket tabloids.

There was a stack of them on the table next to the hair dryer. She had already read them. The same stack sat on her desk at the office. Research. They all had Zara on the cover. Her streaked-blue hair pulled back in a greasy, disheveled bun. Oversized sunglasses covering eyes no doubt swollen from crying and sleeplessness. And the telltale sign of sorrow for a celebrity of her stature: sweatpants.

POP PRINCESS ZARA SINGS BLUES AFTER LIAM SPLIT

INSIDE ZARA'S DEVASTATING HEARTBREAK

**FRIENDS WORRIED SUPERSTAR ZARA
MAY DO SOMETHING INSANE**

That something, apparently, was going mansion hunting in Aspen.

Obviously, Claudine had been shocked when she called. Shocked that it was Zara herself and not a personal assistant. Shocked that someone Zara's age still knew *how* to call. Claudine's younger employees only texted.

"I found the listing for Montague House online," Zara said. Her voice sounded normal, without a trace of the soaring falsetto that had sold out arenas around the world and earned her fifty million Instagram followers. "I'd like to fly in and see it next Thursday."

"Absolutely," Claudine said. "We have our company holiday party that day, but I'll reschedule."

Claudine was relieved. Money was so tight that she'd already scaled back the holiday party from previous years. Usually she hired a top caterer to pass hors d'oeuvres and mix specialty cocktails. This year the plan was takeout: spring roll platters and Thai meatballs. Even the self-serve prosecco bar felt like a stretch.

"Don't reschedule. I can see it another time—" Claudine could hear the waning interest in her voice, Zara was only used to hearing yes.

"We can combine them?" she offered quickly before she had time to think about what she was saying, before she could process how this would affect Henry. "Why don't I move the party to the house. It was absolutely built for entertaining, and you can see it in top shape."

"A holiday party sounds perfect," Zara said. "It's so hard to get in the spirit in L.A. And being around people right now would be good for me. What can I bring?"

For a moment Claudine almost didn't tell her about the White Elephant. She could just cancel it. Her employees would be glad. She knew how much they dreaded it each year. At most holiday parties, the game was a lighthearted romp. Cheap gag gifts. Ten- or twenty-dollar limit. Claudine's version was different. In introducing the annual game, she had neglected to include a price limit. After a couple years, a spirit of one-upmanship had been established, along with an expectation that each employee should bring a lavish gift, one that reflected how well they'd performed over the year, how much they'd racked up in commissions. The purpose had originally been to make people laugh, to reward the most clever. After a few years of observing the tradition, however, it was clear that their lighthearted, team-building holiday game served only to create competition, cause jealousy, and stir rivalry among her staff. Claudine encouraged a level of competition, but even she would admit that including Zara in this year's White Elephant would make the team even more uneasy and desperate to impress.

"Ooh, I love party games!" Zara said. "Entertaining is my jam, and it'd be nice to see the space full of people."

Having it at the house posed a few problems. Sure, it was available. That wasn't an issue. Mr. and Mrs. Lions—the first and only owners—had already moved to Scottsdale. And the place was still furnished. The moving company wasn't coming until after the holidays. But switching the party from the office to Montague House meant Claudine would have to make it a more extravagant affair. Catering. Florals. A piano player would be a nice touch, given the Lions' gorgeous black Steinway grand. She'd need to invite a few more people to fill out the space. And invitations. No matter how intimate, a proper soirée required a proper invitation. Claudine was willing to make certain compromises, but not when it came to etiquette.

The biggest problem was Henry. He had been so distraught over her taking the listing. Of course, he didn't come out and say so. Too quiet. Never said much of anything. She was the talker, the salesperson. He expressed himself through his designs. Yet it was hardly a coincidence that right after she told him the Lions had asked her to sell Montague House, he wound up in the hospital. She knew what the mention of the house must have stirred up. The unspoken. If business wasn't so bad, she wouldn't have dared—would have told the Lions to find another broker. They did not have that luxury. They couldn't refuse any listing. At least it was one of theirs. If things didn't pick up soon, Claudine would have to consider branching into listings for houses Henry hadn't designed. That the Alpine brothers hadn't built. That Calhoun + Calhoun hadn't overseen from the dig to dinner with the new owners.

Taking the listing was one thing. Asking Henry to come to the party at Montague House was another. He hadn't been back since they finished building it and turned the keys over to the Lions. He wouldn't even drive past it, taking long detours to avoid catching the slightest glimpse of the property. To go back there after all these years, to once again step through those large oak doors into the marbled foyer, into the past . . . who knew what that might do to him?

In just a few hours, they would find out. She didn't ask Henry to go. She *told* him he was going. She needed him there in order to make this sale. No one could explain the home's many intricate features better than the man who'd designed them. Besides, the name of the company was Calhoun + Calhoun. Surely Zara would be offended if only one Calhoun could bother to be present.

There was simply no overstating the importance of tonight. It had the potential to change everything. Selling Montague House to an A-lister like Zara would solidify Claudine as the town's most exclusive agent, placing her once and for all ahead of Steve. This sale would leave him and his company in the dust. Imagine the inquiries she'd get. Calhoun + Calhoun's client base would soar. The deluge of calls and emails. The boost to their social media. Right now they only had three thousand or so followers. How many would they add with one shot of Montague House on Zara's Instagram and @calhounandcalhoun tagged? Fifty thousand? A hundred thousand? Good god, what if Zara took a selfie of the two of them and posted *that*? What was she doing at this cut-rate salon? What would a few hundred dollars more matter to her overdue Amex balance? Visionaries didn't compromise.

Claudine put the guest list into her purse and picked up one of the magazines to memorize a few more details about Zara and her recent breakup with heavily tattooed goth rocker Liam Loch.

One of the biggest questions is who will get custody of Pip, the cute rescue Pomeranian that Zara and Liam adopted shortly after they started dating.

Claudine hoped it was him. She hated dogs. She didn't need that fur ball running around Montague House, shedding everywhere, pissing in the corners. Small dogs especially were attention suckers.

She had to admit, there was something poetic about the entire situation. Zara was obviously hoping Montague House would be a new chapter, a fresh beginning—just like it had been for Claudine. That five-acre plot of land had rescued her, set her life on a different trajectory. Now all these years later it would serve the same purpose for Zara.

She checked the time on her Cartier Tank Anglaise: 2:45 p.m. She was supposed to meet the caterer at Montague House at 5:00 p.m. No time for lunch. Not like she had planned on it, she hadn't been eating much the past few days. There were leather Balenciaga pants to fit into. After the salon, she'd hurry back to the office to check in with her staff, change into her outfit for the night, and grab her White Elephant gift. She had to say, in all her years of the game, it was maybe the best gift she'd ever chosen. Not the most expensive, but likely to draw the most gasps.

She tossed the magazine back on the pile, reached once more into her purse, and took out the thin wooden invitation. Made from reclaimed wood salvaged from last summer's fires near Basalt and embossed with gold-leaf lettering:

Cocktails + Hors d'oeuvres 6 p.m.
White Elephant Exchange 7 p.m. Sharp

There was a festive touch of deep cranberry stain around the edges. Later on, when reporters were interviewing the guests and trying to put together a timeline of the night, Captain Tiggleman would say they should have known something was terribly wrong from the beginning. Even the invitation looked like it had been dipped in blood.

Zara

I want to go on record saying I was not the one who brought that gift to the party. It couldn't have been me. Look at the facts: I'd only flown in that day, I'd never met any of these people, and I didn't know what a White Elephant game was until Claudine told me. Sure, yes, I brought *a* gift; we all did. That was the point. But no way did I bring *that* gift. Don't even think it.

See, this was a really weird time for me even before what happened that night. It was right after my breakup with Liam. Six months we'd been together. Personal record. I know that's longer than most people thought we would last. I was twenty-three. He was thirty-four. Which meant together we were fifty-seven, exactly how old Prince was when he died. I was a former Disney TV child actor turned red-hot pop sensation. He was a shock rocker who'd been mentored by Marilyn Manson and boycotted by conservative religious groups. I didn't have a single tattoo. He had thirty-two—thirty-three if you count the one he got of my name on his left bicep. Though I saw he recently changed it to Zarathustra, which I guess is some book by this mopey old philosopher dude that has a really long Wikipedia page. Does that count as thirty-four, then?

Anyway, people have Liam all wrong. That whole "prince of darkness" thing is mostly a schtick. Yeah, I said it. An act. It's phony. He thinks it's "performance art." Which is why I called it a schtick. Because he is a total asshole and the thought of making him angry makes me very happy. He has no idea what performance art even is. It's an actual thing.

In real life, he's a pretty down-to-earth guy. Likes moonlight drives along the Pacific Coast Highway, rooting for the Dodgers, eating Indian food, and adopting rescue dogs. He already had two pits when we decided to get Pip. It was his idea. He thought it'd be hilarious. Him in his makeup and spooky contact lenses and high-heeled boots walking around with this little poufy Pomeranian. Sometimes I wonder if that's the same reason he pursued me. If it was all just a joke or a prank. People seeing him as the devil corrupting this perfect angel. I admit that was part of the initial appeal for me. I was tired of being thought of as a goodie-goodie. Which is why I decided to dye my hair blue. I wanted to stir shit up. But it doesn't matter how it started, because feelings got real. Fast. Most relationships in Hollywood are publicity stunts. Not this one. I'm sure about that. And Liam would say the same thing if you asked him.

That would mean actually getting him to come out of his house to ask him. There were definitely parts of his public persona that were genuine. Dude keeps serious vampire hours. Blackout curtains. Sleeps all day. And is obsessed with the murder of JonBenét Ramsey. Of course, you know that already. You've seen the giant tattoo on his back, the one that goes from shoulder blade to shoulder blade of her smiling that pretty, perfect pageant smile. Duh, I know: *Maybe that's what attracted him to you, Zara. Young, driven, innocent.* Trust me, that's the first thing I thought of when he hit on me that night at the Grammys after-after-party at the Chateau Marmont. In fact, I called him out. I'd had a few drinks and was clutching my Album of the Year statuette close when I told him, "Don't even think about trying to fulfill your perverted dead-girl sicko fantasies with me." At first he laughed. I don't think he expected that kind of attitude from me. Then he got real serious. Said there was nothing the least bit sexual about his interest in JB. To him, she represented the innocence of the world and how senseless and violent and vicious and evil humanity can be. And the injustice of it all—it sickened him that her killer had never been caught.

That surprised me. I hadn't known much about the case. I mean, how would I? I was less than a year old when it happened. I figured someone had gone to jail for killing her a long time ago. Liam said I should come over to his house in Malibu. We could watch JB documentaries in his home theater until the sun came up. It would be an important part of my education.

"Sounds like a romantic first date," I said.

He laughed again.

"First date, huh? In that case, I have something much better in mind."

Dodgers game followed by Indian food followed by moonlight drive to Malibu house. But no JB documentaries. It wasn't until we'd been together about four months that I finally asked to watch them. He didn't mention it, I'd like to think because our relationship had started to restore his faith in the goodness of humanity and he was focused on our future rather than some random dead girl's past. But I was curious. We didn't spend the night together very much—like I said, his sleep schedule was like Prince Lestat's—but when we did share the same bed, he'd turn onto his side, and there would be JB staring at me with those huge saucer eyes. *What exactly happened to you?* I needed to know.

Big mistake.

Liam had a whole library of JB footage. I'm talking dozens of VHS tapes. (He had to explain to me what VHS was. I'd never heard of it before. The eighties were so weird.) Most of them were those cheesy true-crime network TV shows that only run on Saturday night. We watched all of them. Both of us were in between albums and tours, so we didn't have much else to do. And for Liam it was research. He was planning to write an epic concept album based on JB which he would release on December 25, 2021—the twenty-fifth anniversary of her death. He saw the album as his magnum opus, the work that would define his career and cement his artistic legacy. He wasn't going to announce it. He would drop it that night and surprise his fans. "Just like JonBenét had been surprised by her killer," he told me, swearing me to secrecy. Oops.

The more we watched, the more I was convinced—knew, the family was somehow involved. So obvious. Liam raged against my theories; he thought it was an outsider. Hours and hours we'd argue, each of us getting firmer in our conviction.

"What about the autopsy report?"

"Forget the autopsy report. The key is the 9-1-1 call."

"Okay, well, what about the ransom note?"

"What about it? Faked obviously."

"The boot print."

"Three words: Burke Fucking Ramsey."

Back and forth we'd go. Neither of us could let it go. I don't know why. It was literally so stupid. We'd start raising our voices in exasperation and then the two pits would start barking, which would cause Pip to start yipping her head off until one of us picked her up and stormed out of the room. This happened often.

Then one night I got a text.

Zara, I'm afraid this isn't going to work. I've enjoyed our time together but I can't be with someone who sees the JB case the way you do. Pip should stay with you. It's only right.

You believe that? Dude can strip naked in front of a crowd of thirty thousand people and make himself bleed onstage but doesn't have the balls to break up with me in person. I won't lie. I was devastated. I stopped showering, just threw on sweatpants and put my hair in a gross, greasy bun whenever I had to leave the bungalow I rented in Santa Monica, which I tried to do as little as possible. I stayed inside bingeing on other true-crime documentaries. It was like a cleansing. I wanted to get the image of JB out of my head and figured the best way to do that was to fill it with images of other horrendous crimes. It sounds weird, I know. But, like I said, I was pretty wrecked. Not much from that time makes sense.

When I wasn't watching Investigation Discovery or *48 Hours* or *Dateline*, I was blowing through every Netflix series and HBO doc I could find. My absolute favorite show was *Power, Privilege and Justice*. It had run for nine seasons through most of the 2000s, and now truTV showed reruns. It was hosted by this dandyish-looking *Vanity Fair* writer named Dominick Dunne and covered a lot of famous cases, like the Menendez brothers and Andrew Cunanan. But there were also really obscure ones I never heard of before.

That's how I first came across Claudine Longet. And that's how I eventually wound up in Aspen with a different Claudine. *My* Claudine.

And Henry. Poor, poor Henry.

Henry

It had been three weeks since the hospital. He wasn't feeling any better.

Turning off the shower, he wrapped a towel around his waist and, with a swipe of his fist, cleared enough fog from the mirror to see his reflection. His salt-and-pepper hair was slicked back, damp. He hadn't been sleeping well. The dark circles under his eyes looked like bruises. Claudine wasn't happy about that. She'd left a tube of her concealer out on the counter of the double vanity. He squeezed a dime-sized amount onto the back of his hand and dabbed it on.

She brought her outfit for the party to the office, efficient to the core, but he decided to go home to change. He hoped a midday shower would give him energy, increase his focus. It didn't. It just made him wet.

Why was she making him go through this again?

Their unspoken pact that had lasted over twenty years, broken without so much as a conversation.

Three weeks earlier, they were meeting a client couple, the

Flynns, at the seasonal Nobu pop-up restaurant at the St. Regis. This would have been their biggest sale in more than a year, an eight-million-dollar chalet near Buttermilk. Claudine had brought the papers and planned for them to sign during dessert. Henry didn't make it that far. Just as they arrived at the restaurant, as he held the door open for Claudine, she told him the Lions had called and asked her to take the Montague House listing—and she had accepted. So casual. Just like that. Like it was no big deal. The moment she said the words, his chest tightened. He barely heard the conversation through the appetizers. All he could do was try to process what she'd told him.

Why was she doing this? Hadn't he done everything she asked? His designs were always getting better, keeping up with the latest technology, staying on the cutting edge of eco-friendly architecture that didn't mar the beauty of the homes. Claudine sold him as a passionate, hands-on designer, one who built his houses side by side with the Alpine brothers. This was what set Calhoun + Calhoun apart from other Aspen realty firms. The clients loved how much Henry cared about his work. Loved meeting him and getting to socialize with such an accomplished architect. He hated it. Despised small talk. Hated schmoozing. The way Claudine paraded him around. Having to sit through godawful dinners like this one with the Flynns. But had he ever complained? Had he ever refused her? In their personal lives as well as in work, never. Claudine didn't want kids and she definitely didn't want pets. Fine. So be it. He loved her. Didn't she love him? If she did, how could she bring Montague House back into their lives? He knew business was hurting, but unearthing their past, and in such a public way, threatened everything, especially the delicate psychic edifice they had spent years constructing.

That was their most impressive structure. The lie. It was more complex and intricate than any home he had ever designed. Now Claudine was about to risk burning it down, setting it ablaze and incinerating them with it.

He couldn't breathe. His left arm had started to tingle. The waiter set down their entrées, and the last thing he remembered was thinking Claudine's eyelashes looked exceptionally long, her lids closing as she blinked.

"Henry?" Her voice was behind a veil.

Then blackness.

When he came to, the paramedics were standing over him. He was sprawled among the food and plates that had crashed to the floor, and the Flynns had gone home. The blank look on Claudine's face. That look. What a disappointment he was. She didn't ride in the ambulance. Didn't even come to the hospital until the following morning. Said she'd been trying to salvage the sale. No luck. The scene he'd made had tainted the deal. That didn't surprise him. That was Aspen. It was all about keeping up appearances.

"You didn't even have a heart attack," she said brusquely. Even in sickness he had fallen short. She stood over his hospital bed, not bothering to take off her coat. Burberry? Chanel? Diane Von Whoever? He could never tell them apart. Could never tell why that designer stuff meant so much to Claudine. She'd look beautiful wearing a burlap sack. He knew she wanted to leave as quickly as possible, couldn't stand being around so much frailty and weakness, so many suggestions of her own mortality. "Just stress. A simple panic attack. You're fine."

"No I'm not," Henry said. "You know I'm not. I haven't been for a long time."

That was all they said about it. Which was still more than they had ever said about it.

No part of him wanted to go to this holiday party, tonight. On the bed she had set out what she wanted him to wear. A green crushed-velvet jacket and black bow tie. Instead, he went to the closet and picked out a black cashmere turtleneck—a small act of defiance. She'd sworn to him, after they had sold it to the Lions all those years ago, that he would never have to go to Montague House again. It wasn't the first time she'd lied to him; that was his initial thought. But that wasn't entirely true. She never lied about Steve. She didn't have to. Henry never confronted her about him.

Instead he started drinking. Twenty-three years after he gave it up, could he ever use a shot right now. Something to give him the courage to walk back into that house.

Maybe it was a good thing. Maybe being there was just what he needed. Maybe it would be cathartic. Seeing the staircase, the chandelier, each and every detail he had so carefully chosen and crafted—maybe it would bring back memories of what exactly happened that night after they pulled up to the cabin and his mind went blank. That was the worst part. He couldn't remember anything. All he had were the newspaper reports and Claudine's version. Nothing else. Just a total vacuum. All these years he had to fill in the blanks, and maybe what actually happened wasn't as bad as what he imagined. It couldn't be any worse.

Yes, he needed to look at it like this. That going back to Montague House would give him answers. Be some final step that makes him whole again. He had tried just about everything else. Served on the board of the local Habitat for Humanity chapter. Started an after-school architecture program at an underserved high school. Yet no amount of charitable work provided a feeling of absolution. There was no path to redemption. Of course, there was one thing he hadn't tried: confessing. But he couldn't do it. Placing that burden on someone was selfish. He had altered enough lives. And, more important, confessing would expose Claudine. Implicate her, when she had only been trying to help. Only looking to protect him. He was willing to suffer if that meant she didn't have to. That secrecy was why he couldn't do AA. Step 5: "Admitted to God, to ourselves, and to another human being the exact nature of our wrongs." No problem on those first two. But to another human being? Impossible.

He wandered into the living room and stared at the black-and-white wedding photo that hung above the mantel. A lifetime ago. Their laugh was hard and real, neither looking at the camera. Her head thrown back, eyes closed. Her hair was long, wild with curls, perfectly tangled. He was holding his stomach, face full of laughter, his eyes closed, too, his head finding temporary relief on her shoulder. What was so funny? Had he said it or had she? Another memory lost.

There was one more possible solution he hadn't tried. He realized it lying there in the hospital. It was so obvious. Hard to believe he hadn't thought of it before. Sell the business. Or don't even sell it. Just abandon it. Just don't show up to the office one day. Quit Aspen. Quit Colorado. Hell, quit the country. Thousands of days hadn't made him feel any better. Maybe thousands of miles would. He and Claudine amid a new landscape, new people, a new routine. They could slow down, breathe. Rest. Wasn't that what the doctor had recommended?

This was the dirty art of aging. He'd been spending so much time with Jules at the office lately, it was hard not to compare how thirty years look between faces. The soft glow of Jules's young skin hadn't been tortured with years of fighting internal demons. His name was on more than one of the deep lines near Claudine's left eye, knowing it was a result of her selflessness, internalizing too much responsibility for what was Henry's crime. But still, convincing Claudine would be hard. She refused to admit they were getting older, indulged in cutting-edge facials, and every week drank bottles of collagen. She certainly had no interest in retiring. This whole ordeal with the pop star proved how hell-bent she was to turn things around. Aspen and the business—that wasn't just Claudine's identity; it was her destiny. Henry knew that was how she saw it. How she *had* to see it in order to justify all that had happened to get them there.

He tried to bring up his plan that morning. It went as well as expected.

"Why don't we go somewhere?"

"You know we can't afford a vacation right now."

"I don't mean a vacation. I mean, why don't we go somewhere for good? Leave Aspen."

If Claudine was having an emotion about what he just said, her face wasn't processing it. Then a small sigh of disappointment escaped her, and she said, "Pull yourself together, Henry. You're needed tonight."

Why couldn't he say what he really wanted? *Help me, Claudine. You saved me once. I need you to save me again—for good this time.*

"And don't forget your White Elephant gift," she said before leaving.

That ridiculous game. The way she tried to use it to create a power struggle among their staff and retain her dominance. Henry always hated it, and even more so now, after being in the hospital, fearing for his life, realizing what was important and what wasn't. The mention of the White Elephant made him even more resolved to get out. No, it wouldn't be easy to convince Claudine. But there was no choice. He would have to prove that to her. He grabbed his gift and left for the office. This would be his last year picking a number.

Zara

How had the Aspen murder of Spider Sabich at the hand of beautiful French pop starlet Claudine Longet been forgotten? There was no podcast. No Ryan Murphy series. Just that *Power, Privilege and Justice* episode, which I watched like five times. What a rich mess it all was, a town full of movie stars and moguls, pearls and parties. Traces of cocaine. A rumor of relationship problems. An inadmissible diary. Unreal. Let me set the scene.

It's the 1970s. Spider Sabich (real name Vladimir) is a golden-boy pro skier with blond locks and a winning smile. Sexy, fast, fearless. Former world champion and Olympian. He falls in love with Claudine Longet, this beautiful Parisienne who had moved to America a decade or so earlier to become an actor but first was a Vegas showgirl. It was there in Sin City that she met Andy Williams. Andy was a really popular singer— sort of a more square Sinatra. He had like a TV variety show and was especially beloved for his Christmas albums. Andy and Claudine got hitched and her singing career took off. I know how this business works and there's a lot of nepotism. But in Claudine's case she deserved it. She released a few albums, some with these really melancholy, ethereal covers of songs by the Rolling Stones, Joni Mitchell, and the Beach Boys. Sounds a lot like what Nico was doing with the Velvet Underground or what Brigitte Bardot was doing with Serge Gainsbourg. Claudine was just as gorgeous and fashionable—short skirts, tall boots—but maybe because she was married to a more strait-laced guy like Andy she never got the same cool-kid cred.

She and Andy had three children and were married for like thirteen years, then divorced in the mid-seventies. That's when she hooked up with Spider. Moved with the kids into his mansion in Starwood. Which was like Aspen's version of Beverly Hills. Seemed like a sure second chance for love, but it turned deadly. One night, with all the kids in the house, Spider was shot dead with a replica World War II pistol. That is a real fact. Claudine said it was a horrible accident. They were in the bathroom. She was just showing him the gun, or he was teaching her how to use it? Anyway, it went off. He died on the way to the hospital. She was charged with manslaughter and the trial became national news. On the cover of *People* and everything. Andy was by her side the whole time, walking her in and out of the courthouse. "She needs me very much right now," he told the magazine. "I'm going to be as supportive as I can." He had nothing but nice things to say about Spider. But, there was hot gossip. Seems Spider had been preparing to end things; lately their relationship had been stormy. The police even seized her diary, which supposedly contained a lot of details that didn't make her look very good. It was thick with anxiety. The court ruled it inadmissible, though, and after a four-day trial Claudine was convicted of negligent homicide, a misdemeanor, and given like a twenty-five-dollar fine and thirty days in jail, which she could do "at a time of her own choosing."

I read everything I could about the trial. Bought a copy of that *People* on eBay and even paid for a subscription to the *New York Times* to access their digital archives. I really hated giving them money, since their review of my first album was a total hit piece, but I had to know everything I could about this woman. Whenever anyone thinks of Aspen, they always think of that old, dead dude Hunter who they shot out of a cannon and his flameout pirate sidekick Johnny who—ew, gross—tried to mack on me once in London at a Soho House. But those guys are boring compared to Claudine Longet. Not only did she beat a murder rap, she then married one of her defense lawyers. You can't get more gonzo than that.

Then? Crickets. There isn't much out there about her life after the trial. That's because Spider's family filed a civil suit against her. She settled it out of court, with the agreement that she would never give an interview or write a book about her story (which is its own tragedy).

The one place I could still hear her voice was on her albums. A few were on Spotify but I tracked down all the vinyl. I lit candles and slow-danced by myself on top of the Santa Monica rental's kitchen counters.

My favorite was *Love Is Blue*. Listening to it was like gently spreading out your existential crisis as if it were a leisurely picnic lunch. It made me feel better about losing Liam. It made me feel less alone. And thinking about Claudine still living in Aspen, growing old, made me desperately want to be there too.

So I hopped on Zillow and was like, "Show me my new home in Aspen, please." That's how I found Montague House.

Montague House

Rare find. Sold by original owner. Luxurious seven-bedroom, ten-bathroom modern Swiss chalet atop high mesa flats. Remarkable panoramic views of all four ski areas and downtown Aspen. Thoughtfully designed by esteemed architect. Open floor plan. An art lovers delight with vast walls and vaulted ceilings. Floor-to-ceiling windows. Environmentally conscious construction, built predominantly with locally sourced materials. Four indoor fireplaces. Billiards room. Screening room. Generous outdoor areas. Tiered decks. Hot tub. Firepits. Perfect for both solitude and entertaining. | $18,995,000 | 15,000 SQ FT

The pictures were incredible. Majestic. And, most important, so very different than the place I was living. Being on tour, which is where I usually am, means not being home. Which means not having much furniture. My house was beautiful but cold. Lots of mid-century modern furniture, but not enough throw blankets. This may sound pathetic, but this Montague House looked like it could take care of me. A place where you never had to wear shoes; you just ran around sliding from room to room on wooden floors in fuzzy socks. Yes! This could take all the pain away. Looking at those pictures, I knew it had been built with a caring hand. I needed a caring hand. I clicked the "Contact Agent" button.

That's when I saw the Realtor's name.

Claudine.

Her name was Claudine Calhoun. I freaked out. It couldn't

have been a clearer sign. I didn't even wait for my assistant to come in, I called myself. It was on. I'd see the house, experience some holiday cheer, and immerse myself in Aspen. I was even excited about the White Elephant game. It sounded fun. Now all I had to do was decide what to bring.

But believe me, it wasn't *that*.

We were only together for a few months, but what we had was true love.

I'd met him his third day in town. Though, technically, I saw him on the street the day before. Walking down Galena, him on one side, me on the other. The sun was out and he was squinting, brushing his thick black hair from his face. He looked lost. And beautiful. I figured he was a young actor bound for movie stardom, in town to pay his respects to the older celebrities who'd moved here. He turned and ducked into a hardware store, and I thought maybe I wouldn't see him again.

Then the next day, during one of spring's famous flash downpours, he came into the diner for cover and coffee. That was all it took. Conversation came easy. He was on a sort of seasonal circuit, moving from state to state, mostly harvests, but was lucky to be brought on as an all-purpose hired hand sort of role. Maintaining the property. He was bunking up at Mr. Miller's place on high flats. I only met Mr. Miller a few times; he was quiet, old. Seemed grateful to have Tommy.

This was when, foolishly, I still believed in good luck.

Zara

The idea had been to go alone, but my manager insisted I needed at least one of my bodyguards. Dave volunteered, since it was around the holidays and the other guys have families. He's good at his job, definitely looks the part. He's almost seven feet tall, always wears a custom-made dark suit from some big-and-tall shop. I watched him scoop up two people in each arm when the barrier broke last year when I was main stage at Coachella. Please understand that even though he came with me, I viewed this as a solo expedition of recovery and discovery. Of course the one thing Dave couldn't save me from is if our little plane smashed into a mountain. Which seemed like a real possibility. The turbulence started the minute we left L.A. and never once, not even for a minute, let up. Halfway through I could hear Dave mumbling something like a prayer.

"Are you alright?" I asked.

"I'm usually the bus guy," he said. "Not the plane guy."

Luckily, Pip was there for emotional support, proving once

again that dogs are the only option for a true relationship. The turbulence didn't seem to bother her one bit. She just curled up against my chest in her little sling sack all cuddly and kissing my face. I popped an extra Xanax but didn't manage to sleep. Too much thrashing.

No one warned me that the Aspen/Pitkin County Airport was a teeny-tiny shit landing strip wedged between the Rocky Mountains. It dared planes to land, like preteens dared each other to make out in a closet, all angst ridden and secretly hoping it will all be over fast. When we finally landed, everyone clapped louder than opening night at *Hamilton*. (Which reminded me, I owed Lin a text. He'd been so sweet to reach out after the breakup, but I hadn't wanted to talk to anybody.) Later at the party, the Tigglemans told me the airport cancels a third of all flights because of safety and that they were surprised I got in given the conditions. WTF.

My schedule keeps me chasing the sun. Usually I'm just popping from summer festival to summer festival around the globe, so snow and I don't have a ton of history. That's why I wasn't sure if it was normal that these Aspen flakes were the size of my hand. By the look of everyone rushing around so much, I was guessing not. I was guessing this snow was pretty intense. Pip was loving it. She thought the flakes were chew toys. She kept trying to bite them as they were falling.

I was totally underdressed. Even in the airport, the Aspen women were really bringing it. In the short walk through the terminal I counted three pairs of Jimmy Choo shearling boots, two Pucci down coats, and a dozen skintight bodysuits. I had showered for a change and was actually wearing jeans rather than the post-breakup sweats, but my Air Force 1s were the closest thing I had to boots, and as soon as I stepped outside, my feet got soaked. Luckily, Dave and I didn't have to walk too far. The Escalade he hired was waiting out front.

I texted Claudine.

Wheels down! Pip and I heading straight to the Hotel Jerome. Desperate for a gimlet. See you at six. oxxo

Claudine

Claudine swirled in her chair as her phone buzzed. Good, Zara had landed.

On Claudine's strict order, the offices of Calhoun + Calhoun were stark white: the exposed-brick walls painted white, white bistro lights, long white tables with white bowls of white chocolate individually wrapped in white. After a bit of negotiating with the building's owner—although it was hardly ever a negotiation with her; more like a swindling, because few stood a chance—Claudine even had the gorgeous wide-paneled oak floors also painted white. Employees were told to keep their desks sparse and hang their coats in the closets, and if they had to eat at all, do so only in the kitchen. Keep it clean.

Her staff understood that Claudine wanted clients walking through the door and seeing their own vision projected on the crisp surfaces. Their personal canvas. To be inspired. Clients respond to the minimalist nature of the office. The employees who knew Claudine best understood another reason for the crisp white offices was that this choice, minimalism, was easiest to defend. Abstract enough to talk about and appealing to both the avant-garde and the traditional. She applied the same philosophy to showing houses. Most agents believed in staging, creating a sense of home, hoping that would tap into a client's sense of comfort, of belonging. Not Claudine. She preferred to keep a house empty, to encourage a prospective buyer to use their imagination—or, rather, for her to impose her imagination on them. Lately this approach had also been a matter of necessity. Staging a home was another expense Calhoun + Calhoun couldn't afford.

Claudine stepped out of her office and summoned her staff. "All right, everyone."

They surrounded her in seconds. Looking around the half circle of attentive faces, Claudine was proud of them. Proud of them because she had picked them. She had curated the team carefully. Purposefully. There was very little she did without purpose. She knew the importance of a balancing act. That creating the right army could be the difference between being basic successful and stinking-rich successful. Every one of their employees had a unique talent that made a noticeable contribution to the business.

Rashida was the listener of the group. The agent for those clients who needed a therapist as much as a new home.

Louisa was the data nerd. She had come from a career in analytics and was brilliant at tracking the latest trends. Most recently, she'd worked on Bernie Sanders's presidential campaign. But after reading a Harvard study that concluded the human life span was longer in Colorado than D.C., she packed her bags and headed west.

Natalie had spent time in the Army Reserve and her fastidiousness made her the agent best suited for the more high-maintenance customers, those who found flaws in every little thing. She could anticipate their issues before even they could and steer them out of sight.

Alice was the landscape expert—the agent for those who cared more about what surrounded a house than the house itself.

John was the agent for the old divorcées, the ones whose husbands had abandoned them for a newer model and who were eager to drop their hefty settlement on a place unsoiled by infidelity. Maybe John would like to move in with them, they'd joke. He'd laugh and flirt—and more, Claudine guessed, given the constant rotation of Rolexes and Omegas and TAGs on his wrist. He wasn't doing *that* well in sales. None of her agents were. Not lately.

Given the firm's struggles, she knew they must have thought it odd when a few months earlier she had hired Jules. Her yoga instructor. Jules wasn't tasked with any significant responsibilities. Managing the office, ordering pens and Post-its and other supplies, doing errands. She was good at her job, and things did seem to work more smoothly with her around. The agents were happy they no longer had to run out for their own coffee. They weren't complaining. Certainly not to Claudine directly. Never. In private, though, they probably assumed that Jules's hiring had more to do with the one-on-one midday yoga sessions she gave to Claudine in the smaller conference room that was never used. The staff knew their boss well, taking Jules off the market assured her the best personal trainer in town. She didn't like to share.

At least they knew *one* of their bosses. Henry, on the other hand, not so much. Claudine knew they saw him as an enigmatic artist—nice enough but shy, introverted, a bit socially awkward. Their jobs called for little interaction with him. Recently he remodeled the office, putting his office on the other side of the space from Claudine's. Sometimes the agents could go an entire day without seeing him. Since he'd come back from his health scare and grown even more withdrawn, they were giving him a wider berth than usual.

Except for Jules. She and Henry had a connection. In the weeks prior to the hospital and the Flynn deal imploding, she had been staying at the office late, helping him with paperwork for the project. Claudine was surprised. Jules didn't seem like Henry's type—the antithesis of herself. Sweet, smiley, and zero style. She wouldn't deny she had a slight twinge of jealousy, even though Henry was certainly within his right to stray, what with her and Steve. She knew he wouldn't. He preferred his self-pity and self-righteousness to a fleeting office tryst. And Claudine was glad for that, because that self-loathing was what made his work so damn good. His designs were fueled by those feelings. The worse he felt, the more attention to detail there was. It was the only thing that offered him an outlet. An escape. Especially after he gave up drinking. Now, since the hospital, it didn't. He wasn't able to work at all. And so, more than feeling jealousy toward his connection to Jules, Claudine felt relief that Henry had a new distraction. A harmless flirtation to keep him from spiraling too deeply into whatever was going on in that brilliant head of his. But he was off. What was he thinking, just that morning talking about leaving Aspen for good? It was foolish. And on this day of all days, with Zara in town and the fate of the company at stake.

"I'm heading to Montague House a touch early," Claudine told the semicircle of agents. "I need all of you to be there at the very least thirty minutes before. This is the biggest night of your life. Everything—every mini–crab cake, each piece of imported chocolate—is about closing the deal. Never, not even for a moment, forget that tonight is about that one thing. It's not over until Zara is Aspen's newest resident. Whatever it takes."

Do what it takes, or you'll be left behind. One of the many tips she had taken from Steve. It was good advice. He had plenty of that. How to run a flawless open house, the best way to flatter a potential client without sounding like a kiss-ass, how to identify a serious buyer from a time-wasting lookie-loo. In the early days, she was like one of those remora fish that attach themselves to the back of a shark, eating the bloody scraps falling out of its mouth. But, unlike those fish, hers hadn't been a free ride. A quick ride, sure. Mercifully, Steve was always quick. And always apologetic about it. Blaming her for being so hot, too much of a turn-on. She'd be lying to say that didn't boost her ego. But that wasn't what she was in it for. It was strictly transactional. Steve got to fuck her, and Claudine got to learn the business quicker than if she'd just bided her time as an agent.

Apparently going back to Montague House wasn't just bringing back memories for Henry. But there was no time for reminiscing.

"If you need motivation," she continued, "just think about how later, when Zara tells the entire world the story of how she fell in love with Aspen, you'll take pride in knowing you played a role. Right, Louisa?"

Louisa jumped to attention from her wall slouch, coffee almost sloshing out of her mug. At least it wasn't the old Bernie one that Claudine had thrown out. It was so tiring, wrangling the progressives.

"Yes. According to a Kelton study, two-thirds of people are influenced by their first impressions," said Louisa. "We need to get it right the first time."

"Louisa," Claudine said, "your job tonight is to collect the coats and purses. I don't want any of the catering staff to do it. I don't trust their sticky fingers."

"I'll stop and buy some extra hangers just to make sure we have enough," Louisa said.

"Obviously, get the sturdy wood kind. Not cheap plastic ones," Claudine said. "Rashida, I want you to keep an eye on the Alpine brothers. They are strictly décor. Their attendance is merely to add local flavor. The only time they should open their mouths is when they are eating. So keep them over by the beef carving station and out of Zara's way."

"Sure thing," said Rashida.

"Alice, have you confirmed the plant delivery?"

"Yes," said Alice. "Everything has arrived. Weeping figs in the entryway, succulents on the coffee tables, butterfly orchid on the mantel."

"John," Claudine said, "two things. One, not too much flirting with Mrs. Tiggleman. A little is okay. We want her to be happy. But too much could upset the captain. We want him happy too. I don't need to tell you, they are both very important clients. And two, I need you to bring party favors. In case Zara's expecting something a bit more . . . exciting."

"Any idea what she's into?"

"Bring an assortment."

"Looks like more snow is in the forecast."

"Are we worried about the actual snow?" asked Rashida. "It's pretty nasty out there. What if the roads start to get too bad. Should we be worried about how Zara will get home?"

"Are you sure you're concerned about Zara and not yourself?" Claudine said.

Rashida looked down in embarrassment.

"Want me to calculate the frequency of snowplows and salt dispersal in this area just to be safe?" Louisa asked.

"No," Claudine snapped. "The weather will *not* ruin this night."

The way she said it was both a guarantee and a threat to the earth's atmosphere.

"Natalie."

"Yes, ma'am." A military habit she couldn't break, no matter how many times Claudine chided her. She despised the formality. It made her feel ancient.

"Natalie, if you call me 'ma'am' tonight in front of Zara, I'll fire you."

"Of course, ma—Claudine."

"You're in charge of quality control. Walk through the house and make sure nothing is out of place. The throw pillows plumped. The central fireplace stoked. All table runners removed."

"We hate table runners," Natalie said.

"The house must look like Aspen's own Windsor Castle."

"You mean Buckingham Palace?" asked Jules.

"No," Claudine said. "The queen weekends at Windsor. Someone like Zara needs many houses. Montague House is the one where, in the middle of her chaotic life—whether she's taking a bow from a stage in Tokyo or fleeing from paparazzi through the streets of Zurich—she'll long to return to, to escape it all."

It was then that Claudine noticed Jules's outfit. A long-sleeved evergreen knit dress splashed with tiny snowflakes.

"You're wearing that?"

"It's festive!" Jules said. Unlike the other agents, she didn't act intimidated by Claudine. She had a youthful composure, but also an air of discipline. It was even evident in her hand-writing. The little notes she left for the agents letting them know of a missed call were so fluid and graceful. It looked almost like calligraphy. And so Claudine had a special task for Jules.

"I need you to write out the White Elephant numbers. In fact, I'm putting you in charge of anything and everything White Elephant related. Make sure the long oak table is arranged in the living room so that everyone can see it. You are to take each person's gift as soon as they arrive. This is important. They are not to place their gift on the table themselves. That would give away who brought what."

"Understood," Jules said.

"Is Zara playing?" John asked.

"Yes," Claudine said. "Two things to keep in mind. One, if she steals your gift, no pouting. *John.*"

"Last year it felt like people were ganging up on me."

"And two, in no scenario ever does one of you steal from Zara. Got it?" Though that wouldn't be a problem since Claudine was handing out the numbers herself. She'd make sure Zara was in the sweet spot.

They all nodded.

Claudine stared past them, through the windows, momentarily mesmerized by the snow. It really *was* coming down hard. Perhaps Rashida had a point. If they wound up snowed in and Zara was forced to spend the night with this collection of odd characters, it would jeopardize the sale. They would have to move the festivities along quickly. Two hours at most. Claudine addressed the group once more.

"Everyone, please remember: yes, tonight we're throwing a party, but this is also work. Enjoy yourself, but not *too* much. Let's keep the drinking under control."

Just then the main door opened and in came a very tired-looking Henry. Barely glancing their way, he took the shortcut through the kitchen to his office.

Henry

God, the brightness of the office hurt Henry's eyes. Between the white walls—the white *everything*—and the sheets of snow coming down beyond the windows, it was blinding. Squinting, he could see Claudine at the far end, their tortured employees surrounding her. He felt sorry for them, which was a relatively new feeling. He used to think of them as the glue that kept the agency together, but recently he could only thank god his office was as far as possible from whatever terrible meeting was happening. From her. He couldn't bear to hear whatever orders they were receiving or her instructions on proper manipulation tactics. In his brief glance, it felt like he was looking through a long tube, him on one side, and all of them smaller and trapped on the other.

He never used to see it, how every word out of Claudine's mouth was in service of her own agenda. Now it was all he saw. Yes, there was more financial stress than ever, but to actually take the listing for Montague House changed everything. They were supposed to never look back. Little truths were piling up, throwing him off-balance. They'd been a team for so long. But had she always been like this? He knew that when you're as close as they were, working together, living together, it can be hard to recognize change. Was it possible he'd never seen who she was?

The hard reality was that they were in one of those stretches that happens in any long marriage. They were on different frequencies, but eventually they'd find each other. They always did. Although today he was glad her office was on the other side of the floor. A key decision he made last year when they'd remodeled—separate heads of the table. Keeping watch from each end. At least, he had thought he believed that; now he wondered if subconsciously he was creating a necessary distance between them—space to be himself.

Sliding off his Sorrels, he put them on the shoe rack inside the door and put on his work slippers. Then, before anyone could call him over, he took a sharp right, cutting through the kitchen, down the hall, to the safety of his office.

Door closed.

Blinds closed.

His phone chirped.

Glad u r back. Feeling better?

Jules. Always so thoughtful. It was barely a secret she had a crush on him. He wasn't going to overanalyze a bright spot in his day, but he knew to be careful. There was a need to make sure that nothing he said or did could be twisted or misunderstood. Also, he wasn't Steve. Jules was safe, and honest. It was fine if her extra attention made him feel better. She was so unlike Claudine. For one thing, she made him laugh. It wasn't his style to form a crush on an employee, and he wasn't going to start now. But he could indulge just enough. Who knew, maybe he was wrong about the way she felt? Maybe she only liked him as a friend, and he was so out of touch, having been married so long, he had no idea what that looked like. On top of everything else, there was no way he'd set himself up for rejection and embarrassment. He walked around with enough shame. But it didn't stop him from spending as much time as he could with her.

It was hard to believe that Jules had worked there only a few months, she kept the place running. The yoga community's loss was Calhoun + Calhoun's gain. Jules told him that she liked having coworkers, the feeling of comradery so different than her usual role of teacher-pupil. It was good to feel connected, in the trenches with everyone, even if her contributions were currently small. She could see a day where she did more, became important.

In recent weeks she and Henry had been staying at the office late, working long into the evening. It was under the auspices of putting more hours into the new property the Flynns had been interested in, but it was obvious they just enjoyed each other's company. For Henry, her lightness was a welcome respite from the intensity Claudine brought to any room she occupied. They'd order takeout, burgers from 520 Grill, and talk about anything but work. Henry would tell her about recent Scandinavian buildings that caught his eye. He admired their unique way of blending energy efficiency with an emphasis on the importance of nature in design. She'd talk about the books she was reading, how she liked to alternate between classics and thrillers. It felt comfortable and familiar as they cycled through subjects, big and small. Who made the best ski pants. The definition of happiness. Are Doritos better than Cheetos.

What about Flamin' Hot Cheetos. Their conversations rolled like a taffy machine, stretching out long and colorful, then folding over and over again until they were all one.

They became close in a way that not even they could articulate. In all these years, it was the nearest Henry had ever come to wanting to tell someone his secret. He'd tease the thought out all the way until the breath before he was going to do it, always stopping short when it came time to form the words. Where would he even start? No. Not ever. Especially not Jules. This wasn't the way to do it. To relieve the symptoms he'd been feeling. The tightness. The pressure. It was as if someone had him by both shoulders, pressing down from above, crushing him like a boot on an empty aluminum beer can. It'd been years since he'd been this tempted to have a drink. His current state was unsustainable.

A light rapping on the office door. Jules cracked it open.

"Hey," she said. "Thought I'd check on you in person. You okay?"

"Just tired. Not exactly in a Christmas party mood."

"Holiday party," she corrected. "We run an inclusive shop here. Wouldn't want to offend a potential client."

"You learn fast."

Jules tucked her hair behind her ears, a nervous habit. It was only then that he noticed her dress. He was confused and a little startled.

"Why are there skulls all over your dress?" he asked her. There were dozens of them. Hundreds. Little tiny skeletons. All just staring at him. He heard them giggle then realized it was Jules.

"Skulls?" she said. "These are snowflakes."

God, Henry thought. *Pull it together. Pull it the fuck together.* He forced a fake laugh.

"Guess I'm due for a trip to the eye doctor."

"Look, I understand what's going on," Jules said.

"No," Henry said. "I don't think you do."

"You're nervous about going back to the house."

Henry was instantly flooded with terror. How could she know? In one of their late-night office conversations, had he slipped up and told her and somehow forgot? It wouldn't have been the first time he forgot something so monumental and life altering. Although what was his excuse in this case, without booze?

"You're worried about seeing your first house. That you're going to be disappointed by it. And that when faced with all the time that has passed since . . . you'll feel old. Skulls? I'm no psychologist, but it seems pretty easy to guess what that means."

Henry laughed, relieved. Yet what she said made a lot of sense. She was wise, not just smart.

"I, for one, am excited," she said. "I can't wait to see the house, Henry." She rarely said his name, and he felt a small thrill. "I've heard so much about it, driven past it, seen all the pictures. I'm sure they don't do it justice. I'm so grateful to have the chance."

And he was grateful she would be there. Buoyed by her presence and her enthusiasm, he might be able to get through this night.

He would do everything that Claudine wanted. He would smile. He would lead Zara on a tour, pointing out unique attributes of the house. As he had done so many times over the years, he would play the brilliant architect for the night. And then tomorrow he would quit. How hard could it be to pretend everything was fine for, what, a couple hours? Make Claudine happy. Sell the house. Sell it and never, ever, ever, ever think of it again. It was a good plan. It was the *only* plan.

"I also can't wait to see your White Elephant gift," Jules said. "I bet it's lavish."

"Don't say 'lavish,'" Henry said. "That's a Claudine word."

Jules smiled but then stopped. Henry wasn't kidding. There was a severe look on his face. He didn't want any part of Claudine rubbing off on Jules.

"Well, I think my gift is going to cause quite a stir," Jules said. "It's been a work in progress almost since I started here. But I landed on something extraordinary. Alice and Natalie were telling me horror stories from the last few years. How people who brought underwhelming gifts weren't around much longer after that. That's why I put so much thought into it. I wanted to be sure I stood out."

You always stand out, Jules. That's what he wanted to say. Why couldn't he? Why couldn't he be that bold? He had walked to the very edge of wherever that imaginary line is drawn between harmless flirtation and pointed seduction. Why couldn't he step across it?

"Claudine," Henry said. "She probably needs you. I'll see you over at Montague House."

Jules smiled and closed the door on the way out.

Soon, when he wasn't at the Miller property, he'd be at the diner. Sitting in a back booth while I worked, drinking coffee. Loved books. Always reading someone's memoir. He'd tell me he liked reading about great lives, since the one he was living was so small. See, he had this whole interior life. If everything hadn't happened, there would have been a lifetime of adventures and discoveries. But he wasn't always so heavy. There was a playful side. He made his own bookmarks from pressed flowers, partial to the wild Aspen sunflowers and hillsides full of purple lupines that blanket Buttermilk.

We made the most of our time, and it makes me smile even now to think of him. This is the way I choose to remember him. I need you to know they were good memories. He took me fly-fishing, on picnics. Sometimes we would just lay a blanket down near Mr. Miller's cabin and take in the view. I'd lived here my entire life and didn't know the place existed! It was gorgeous. You could see a perfect sunset, the whole sky glowing pink and red. The world was on fire.

I've told you how he died. A logging truck collision on the back road.

That is a lie. That's not how he died at all. Forgive me. The truth is much harder to comprehend. Much harder to live with.

Zara

As we rode in from the airport, I realized Aspen was like a perfect toy town, nestled in the mountains. Trees wrapped with lights, branches heavy with snow that looked like frosting. Regal horse-drawn carriages, giant red bows tied around lampposts, people standing at bus stops with their skis. Holiday perfection.

Dave sat up front next to the driver, Pip and I buckled safely in the back seat as we cruised down Main Street. With the weather what it was, it was a smart move having a local driver. Besides, he could call out some fun history along the way. Over there's where silver was first discovered. Right there is where the army trained skiing soldiers for World War II, the 10th Mountain Division. Had I heard of Jerome Wheeler? Aspen's original developer. He built tons of things, like the opera house and our destination, the Hotel Jerome. I didn't care about any of that. There was only one place I wanted to see.

"Where's the courthouse?" I asked.

Burned in my mind was that picture of Claudine Longet and

Andy Williams, miracle ex-husband, walking down the sidewalk, up the steps, a united front. Proof that the only thing that ever mattered happened in the present tense. No one would have blamed him if Andy'd just like stayed in L.A. or wherever he was. But he flew in right away. To be with her. With the kids. They were the picture of solidarity. Her high boots, the double-breasted fitted coat, those gloves. It was everything. Andy held her hand every day as they walked into her murder trial. Pure class.

The driver pulled up in front of the building.

"Take a close look at the statue perched above the main doors," he said. "Notice anything strange?"

I stared at it for a few seconds. I was terrible at puzzles like this. Always hated *Where's Waldo?* I shook my head no.

"Lady Justice is usually blindfolded. Here she isn't. Makes sense when you think about Aspen. We've never had blind justice. No such thing as being impartial. Don't let all these fancy shops and famous people fool you. Always has been and always will be the Wild West."

I got out of the car and walked to the front of the courthouse. There were nine steps up to the main doors. I climbed them trying to imagine what it must've felt like for Claudine back then, wondering if being there gave me more clarity about whether or not she did it. Even after reading so much about the case, I honestly wasn't sure. Did Claudine shoot Spider accidentally or intentionally? With the snow floating down around me, I still had no idea.

I got back in the car and we drove down the block to the Hotel Jerome. They were on the same street.

"You picked the right hotel," the driver said. "Sure, some people like the other hotels here—the St. Regis, Little Nell—but there's only one that has it all. History, celebrity, luxury. From the very beginning. Can you imagine it's been here since 1889? This hotel has seen everything. Prospered during the boom, survived the silver crash, the Depression. The revival. All the revivals. Owners have changed hands more times than I can count. If there's one certainty in Aspen, it's uncertainty. Not much thrives on consistency; it's reinvention. Adaptation. That's good news for you. These days, it's fit for a queen."

When Pip and I walked into the lobby, we knew he was right.

I always love this story I once heard about one of those old queens of England. She wants to know what life is like as an ordinary girl. So she steals clothes from one of her servants' children and runs out of the palace into the countryside. Soon she comes upon another little girl around her same age. They spend the afternoon together, racing each other through the fields and picking flowers and chasing bunny rabbits. Eventually they sit down on a rock wall to catch their breath. A cool breeze brushes the little queen's hair from her face, her cheeks rosy from so much running. A frog hops by.

Then the girl says to the queen, "If you could be anything in the world when you grow up, what would you be?"

The queen looks around. Here they are in the countryside. It's so pleasant. So peaceful. The girl's house is in the distance, at the bottom of a sloping hill. It has a fat thatched roof, and the homemade lace curtains flutter in the breeze. A curl of thin smoke rising from the chimney. The girl's father and mother are surely tucked inside, dinner being prepared, a peaceful night ahead. The girl looks proud as she watches the little queen's face take in all that is her life.

Then the little queen turns to her and says, "I want to be the fucking queen of England."

With that, she pops off that rock wall and skips her way back to the palace.

I know that feeling. The temporary confusion of being famous but wanting to be regular. This is what it's like to be a celebrity. Sure, there are some downsides. Paparazzi. Stalkers. Careless fashion bloggers. It's all worth it. Any famous person who says they wish they weren't is full of shit. Our lives are easy. Drivers, trainers, stylists, personal chefs. We don't have to lift a finger. Walking into the Hotel Jerome was no different. Porters took my bags and the concierge whisked me into the barroom, where the bartender was already pouring my gimlet. I sat close to the fireplace beneath a distorted painting depicting two men in darkness, lit only by the campfire or lantern or whatever. A portrait of roughing it hanging in the middle of all that elegance. And I thought, they must have been here a million times. Claudine Longet and good ol' Andy, popping over for a post-court drink. In the old days people were always doing things like that.

I sipped my gimlet and the warmth from the fire felt nice. Then I scooped Pip up and headed to my room. It was time to dress for the party. Getting ready is always my favorite part. I like to take my time. Crank the music, do my own makeup. I was going to look good, I knew I brought a killer outfit.

Claudine

The moment she stepped into the massive foyer, she knew the night would be unforgettable. They would sell this house to Zara. She was sure of it.

Unlike Henry, Claudine had decided she was looking forward to seeing Montague House again. It felt like a necessary pilgrimage. Everyone always credited him for the brilliant design, but it wouldn't even be there if it wasn't for her. It didn't used to bother her, that no one knew she was the one who had made it happen. Secured the land, convinced the banks, pushed him to get over the nastiness of the acquisition, so he could use his talents to their full extent and create something unforgettable. None of it would have been possible without her.

The first time he took her up to see the view, all those years ago, she knew her future, *their* future, and the property would be linked. It was one of the only remaining lots that rested in the high planes on a plateau jutting out from the mountain, devastating views of the Rockies in all directions. Yes, what had happened was unfortunate, but the history of the West was full of more brutal dealings than this. The point was they left the world more beautiful than they found it by building the crown jewel of Aspen.

It was exciting, as first projects often are, and they'd been meticulous in every stage of planning. Claudine had it sold before it was finished to a couple who, she realized, were probably the same age as she and Henry were now. The Lions, a perfect last name for who they were—she a supermarket heiress, he a movie producer. They were glamorous, the ideal buyers for her first sale. They'd kept in touch over the years, had sent clients their way, which was so important when just launching a business. But now the Lions found the winters too hard; they were too old and forced to seek asylum in Scottsdale. Claudine had been their first call. They remembered how smart she was, that she'd been a ferocious negotiator when they bought the house from her. The Lions insisted she take the listing. She'd found the perfect owners once; she could do it again.

The Lions' taste in furniture was classic Colorado. Rustic but not shabby. Cozy but not casual. An abundance of leather. Claudine chose just enough pieces that tonight's guests would have a place to sit, that the gifts would have a grand table to be displayed, then had the rest of the first-floor furniture put away in upstairs bedrooms.

It was almost time. She was ready. She'd chosen a black silk Alexander McQueen blouse, leather pants, and leopard-print calf hair Manolos that added a few inches to her already tall, slim frame. The jagged lace cuffs and high collar were a tiny bit of punk she knew would appeal to Zara, show they were two of a kind. Topping it off was an art deco locket necklace. She relished the bit of mystery a locket promises, although she kept the inside empty, a reminder to never fall for nostalgia. She and Henry would look good, him in the green velvet jacket she'd laid out, the picture of elegance as they stood in the entrance hall and welcomed their guests, the grand staircase sweeping behind them. The staircase was a point of pride for Henry. He'd modeled it after the stunning one in the capitol in Denver. The marble stairs were low and deep, the curved oak of the hand-rails regal with a polished brass finish on the top.

Claudine went room to room, the house a swirl of activity, observing the last of the party prep. In the kitchen, chefs put finishing touches on hors d'oeuvres, plating the ones that came out cold. Poached shrimp on rice crackers, tiny crudité kabobs. Dessert towers were being built, small bites of indulgence on each tier. One waiter was setting out the cheese straws and bowls of holiday nuts. Another twisting stacks of napkins into a sculpture-like formation. The third weaving in and out of each room, a thin dust towel in each hand, making sure there wasn't a stray particle on any surface. She had told the catering com-pany to send their best-looking group, and they hadn't disap-pointed. They were all in their twenties, with the kind of lean bodies that come from spending most of their time skiing. All of their bustling was underscored by the piano player warming up on the Steinway.

In the living room the bartender was polishing glasses and icing down white wine and champagne.

"My husband will be the one with the salt-and-pepper hair and can't-miss blue eyes. He's sober and I work to keep him that way. We all like a bit of theatre, so please make sure his drinks look like drinks. Serve them in the same glass you would any other cocktail. Understand?"

"Of course."

"I appreciate your discretion."

Since Louisa wasn't there yet, Claudine hung up her own coat, a tiger print Cavalli. It was a pity Zara wouldn't have a chance to compliment it. If the weather had been nicer, post–White Elephant, they would have gathered with hot chocolate around one of the many firepits, the perfect chance to show it off. Oh well, a small glitch in the scheme of things. Nothing would spoil her good mood. She clutched her gift with both hands. The smooth silver paper felt cool. The ivy twisted around like green barbed wire, a substitute ribbon. Jules would be in charge of arranging the other gifts, but with no one else there to see, Claudine personally set hers down front and center on the table.

Henry

He was happy to drive over alone, wanted time in the car to think. To transform into a version of himself that could pull off what he needed to. It would help to conjure up something positive to focus on. Maybe his initials would still be there? He'd carved them in a hidden spot and never even told Claudine, a secret between him and the house. Leaving his mark seemed necessary. Initially he thought of it like an artist signing a painting, but over the years it felt more like how someone signs a confession. The deep cut of the *H.C.* branding both him and the house, making sure neither one forgot what had happened on this spot.

He punched a button to turn on the seat warmer and practiced smiling a few times into the rearview mirror as he drove.

Wonderful to meet you, Zara.

Drumming his restless fingers on the steering wheel, he promised himself to think about it only for a moment. He'd been a Maker's Mark guy . . . the soothing clink of ice cubes in a glass . . . the gentle trickle of the pour. That had been the one good thing to happen after, at least he had stopped drinking.

He was three miles from the house.

Zara, when I built this house, I knew someone extraordinary would live here.

Two miles from the house.

Zara, let me explain how the garden looks in spring, how everything transforms—part of Aspen's magic.

One mile from the house.

This house becomes part of your very being. You will find happiness here, Zara.

With a deep breath he turned off the highway and began winding up the long drive. Snowdrifts high on either side of the road. At first he caught only tiny glimpses of the house through the trees. The top of the stone chimney. The glow of yellow light, illuminating the front wall of windows. With every switchback, more house flashed by, the higher he climbed.

The inevitability of his situation struck him almost as absurd. He was driving toward the one thing he'd spent so much of his life avoiding. Montague House. But he'd also been its creator. So much time given to its design, drafting, drawing, dreaming. Then building, sanding, carving. If he stripped away the emotion attached to the preceding event, there was a dull ache of longing, almost a magnetic pull the closer he got. It was not only the first house he ever completed; it was his best. Every house after was in the shadow of this first great triumph. He'd peaked at his debut. Like love. He believed you only really fall in love one time. Then, if that doesn't work out and you go and fall in love again, you are only falling in love with the memory of the first time you did.

Claudine had been his first. The house his second.

Rounding the last snowbank, there it was in its entirety. Montague House. Enormous, thrusting its beauty confidently into the stormy night, demanding to be admired.

He knew he wasn't going to enter through the front door. To him, a front door was a guest entrance. Even though it meant getting snow on his shoes, he went around to the side and entered through the mudroom, which led to the kitchen. Sneaking in this way would be less jarring than being immediately thrown into the heart of the house. He went in fast and unsentimental, determined to win the first battle of even entering at all. Not yet taking in the room, he automatically hung up his jacket without realizing he hadn't bothered looking for a hook.

His breathing was all right. He wasn't shaking. He could handle this.

Stepping into the kitchen proper, he was reminded how large it was. At once he noticed the steel of the modern appliances. An upgrade that made sense. Lit candles hung from thin wire, floating in every window. Twenty-foot ceilings full of skylights. The rich red of the cherry wood floor, polished like new. The chefs and waiters continued prepping, hardly acknowledging he was there. Bamboo serving trays lined the enormous island in the center, waiting to be filled.

He still knew the floor plan perfectly. Every hall, step, arch, room, closet, pantry, and deck. The view from each of the 164 windows. Another reason he came in through the kitchen: he wanted to see the spot. If he looked through the window, directly in front of the main sink and across a small meadow, he could see the exact patch of forest where they had stood, young, excited, naïve, the first time he brought her here. How old had he been? Twenty-eight? That made her twenty-six. He looked out toward the trees; the grove of Aspens had grown much taller.

"Why are you in the kitchen, Henry?" Claudine asked from the doorway. His brief moment of tranquility was over. She took in what he was wearing. Initially he thought she was about to compliment him. "What are you wearing? I thought I laid out the green jacket and bow tie?" She didn't even try to mask her disdain.

"You did? I didn't see it. This is the turtleneck you got me last year."

This was just like her, to cut him down right when he was starting to feel better.

"At least take the glasses off."

"I'd like to see. I'm wearing the glasses."

"Everyone will be in suits, Henry," she said, ping-ponging between passive putdowns.

"Doubtful, Claudine. The Alpine brothers don't own them. Besides, there's a blizzard."

No part of him wanted to argue with her. There wasn't much time before guests would be arriving, and he wasn't going to spend it getting worked up. He would ignore her. The impatience in her voice was suffocating. He held tight to his secret, telling himself that he just had to get through the night. Just keep wearing that fake smile. Trying it out, he smiled so hard his cheeks hurt. She stared at him blankly.

Maybe he needed a bigger change than he thought. Maybe they were broken. The gap too wide. Maybe quitting the business and leaving town wouldn't be enough. An uneasiness clenched his torso, tightening like a corset.

"Henry, when we're showing Zara the house, be articulate. Don't mumble your words. Diction is important."

Interesting, she was crueler than usual. This was normally when she sucked up, played him like one of her pawns. Relied on him to help make a sale. Usually he liked it. Questions flooded him.

Why was she standing so expectantly?

What did she want him to say?

Was she waiting for him to have a complete meltdown before the night even started?

Well, he wasn't going to give her the satisfaction of having to manage him. No way. Even if this was his last Calhoun + Calhoun soirée. No, he refused to cause a scene before the first guest had even arrived.

"The emerald drop earrings were a perfect choice," he said instead.

The whistle of a sudden gust of wind howled from outside, a slow whine. The snap of a tree breaking, startling the catering staff in the kitchen. It was one of the taller aspens he'd been admiring a few moments before. He watched as it fell to the ground, swallowed by the snow.

Zara

It's amazing how much snow can fall in two hours. By the time we were on our way to the party, there must have been another three inches. Less cars on the road, less plows. They couldn't keep up. The driver seemed nervous navigating the roads. He had stopped spouting Aspen trivia and was mostly silent. The windshield wipers were on full blast and it didn't even help. We could only see like two or three feet max.

Hoping to help us all relax, I had Dave plug in my phone and I tapped open Spotify. I know Spotify is kind of evil. It takes like a trillion plays to make any real money. Which is fine for artists like me—the math works in my favor—but up-and-coming artists get fucked. On the other hand, it's pretty incredible to have just about every album ever recorded right there in your pocket. And it's awesome to think that some young kid living in the middle of nowhere could randomly stumble on an album like Claudine Longet's *Love Is Blue*. I hit "play" on her soft, magical song "Snow" and asked Dave to turn it up.

It's all over and you're gone
But the memory lives on

What was Liam doing at that very moment? Was he eating Indian food and watching JB docs with some other girl? I had to stop thinking about him. It's strange how certain people who are clearly no good for you can have such a powerful hold. Later on, I would ask myself the same questions about Henry and Claudine. What was it about her? Why was he so hung up? Because by the time I met them, it seemed that any trace of what brought them together initially was gone. Which is depressing. I guess that's just the nature of love. It doesn't make sense. You can never explain it. That's why, of all those millions and millions of tracks on Spotify, probably more than half are about romance and heartbreak and desire. Writing songs about that stuff is the closest anyone can come to figuring it out.

We started making our way up a private drive. As we drove, every few feet on either side of the road were flickering gas lanterns leading us. It almost felt like we were driving up to some sort of bizarro winter finale of *The Bachelor*.

I felt the house before I saw it. Could feel its presence. Ever since I started seeing my Transcendental Meditation guru a few months earlier, I had been more in tune with auras and celestial vibrations. And I have to admit, the house was putting off some wild energy. It loomed on the mountain above, hard to make out at first, then an outline of a fortress. Wood and stone and glass, the largest picture windows I'd ever seen. It was magnificent, but it definitely made me feel a little uneasy. I should've listened more to that instinct. I should've told the driver to turn around and take me back to the hotel and spent the rest of the night snuggling with Pip in bed and ordering room service. But I just chalked up that nervousness to how I usually feel when I'm about to meet total strangers, and how weird and awkward they usually get. It was too late, I was all in.

Around here, if you don't have money, you're nothing. No voice, no one protects you. You become insignificant.

Tommy and I dreamt about the future all the time. About getting out of Aspen. These long, wild talks about the places we wanted to go. They were completely impractical, but that was the point. He had a vision. We'd start in Alaska, spend time camping on the glacial lakes, breathing the sharp, clean air. Then we'd hop a whale-watching boat and cruise down to Seattle, where a car would be waiting for us. A 1965 powder-blue Mustang. He'd talk about sinking down in the bucket seats as we drove cross country. Through Idaho, Montana, South Dakota. Cruise through Illinois, Indiana, Ohio. Cut up through Pennsylvania and New York and keep going until we were lying on the beach, way up in Maine, eating lobster.

Some nights I'd stay over at Mr. Miller's house. We'd sit on these rocks near the edge of the property, overlooking the valley, and whisper all night long. If it wasn't for a few visible lights from new mansions down below, it could have been anytime in history.

This was only the beginning of the greedy developers and their light pollution. Killing the darkness we'd taken for granted. Some nights I swear I can't even find Ursa Major anymore. Aspen was changing every day. The signs were everywhere. A town like this always is, but it was turning *into something I didn't recognize. I think one of the things that brought Tommy and me together was neither of us was interested in status. Maybe we should have been. A sick fact about our little town is that protection is a privilege extended only to certain members of the community.*

Claudine

By 5:59 p.m. everyone had arrived but Zara.

The guests knew better than to be late to the Calhoun Holiday Party, especially because they'd been discreetly informed of the surprise guest. The Alpine brothers, Jack and Bobby, were the first. Their rugged handsomeness full Colorado. They cleaned up well. Henry was right, no suits. Flannels and Carhartt. It worked. They were already crowded around the beef-carving station chatting with Rashida.

Captain and Mrs. Tiggleman arrived next. They moved slowly, both in their late seventies. He had the chiseled profile of an Old Hollywood movie star, and her plastic surgeon had done admirable work. Already their chief concern was the weather. They began talking about it the moment they walked through the door. Louisa took their coats and Natalie whisked them off to the bar, assuring them a cocktail would soothe their worries.

"Nothing melts snow like whiskey," said Captain Tiggleman, which made no sense at all.

Kevin and Jerry were the last to arrive. Henry looked relieved to see his old friends. They were active in the community, involved citizens, which was always good for cocktail conversation. And business. They were regulars at community council meetings and always up with what was happening at the Wheeler Opera House or Theatre Aspen. Plus occasionally they could be helpful, providing inside information about permits and zoning. Kevin worked for the tourism board and had close ties to the Planning and Zoning Commission, and Jerry tended the gardens at the John Denver Sanctuary. They were excited to see Henry, giving him giant hugs, until Kevin pulled back, worried.

"Ah, we should be more delicate," Kevin said. "How are you feeling?"

"Better."

"Such a scare."

"Sorry we were almost late, Claudine," Jerry said, handing her a garish poinsettia. "The car got stuck in our driveway."

"This is beautiful," she said, handing the plant off to a nearby Jules and whispering, "Get rid of it." Jules also took their two White Elephant gifts and left, arms full, to place them on the table.

"The car got stuck," said Kevin. They were always repeating each other. "Shovels, Triple A, the whole thing."

"You wouldn't believe how hard it's coming down outside. I'm so sorry."

"We're so sorry. Shovels and everything. Did Zara get in okay? Is she still coming?"

"Yes," Claudine said. "She should be here any minute."

Then she addressed the entire room. "Excuse me, everyone,

please join me in the living room. There are a few things I'd like to go over before our guest of honor arrives."

They followed one by one to the living room, the exact location where the White Elephant exchange would be held. Claudine had to admit it, Jules had done a great job arranging the gifts on the table. There was a perfect distribution of shapes and sizes, a yogi's sense of proportion. The ideal balance of wrapping paper pattern and color. In the first year or two of the White Elephant, she had had to chastise her employees for imperfectly folded corners and excessive Scotch tape, but no longer. They took much more care with the presentation—or, more likely, paid a professional to do it. Each gift had been wrapped with great extravagance, gold and silver, red and green—the shiny, shimmering wrapping paper reflecting the soft glow of candlelight that took ten years off everyone's faces. Twenty off Mrs. Tiggleman's because of all the work she had done.

The room was inviting, with oversized chairs and deep couches. Sleek vases of holly and ivy. The antique grandfather clock that Henry had cleverly built into the wall. One of the first elite settlers brought it over the Rockies tied to a wagon. By the time Henry found it in an estate sale, it hadn't worked in years. He had it restored to its original glory and built it into a huge bookshelf covering the wall opposite the fire. A permanent fixture of the house and a nod to the settlers who had come before.

Surveying the group, she was quite pleased. Everyone looked sharp, even the hired help. The waiters and bartender dressed chicly in fitted black button-downs and tapered black pants. The chef's whites were starched and as yet unstained.

The piano player's tuxedo was obviously one he owned and not a rental, the bow tie actually tied, wasn't a tacky clip-on. With the exception of Jules's ridiculous snowflake dress, the Calhoun + Calhoun staff looked fashionable. And although Henry would've looked better in the green jacket, he looked distinguished. He stood slightly off to the side, at the back of the group. *Fine,* Claudine thought, *let him play his favorite role: reluctant participant.* At least he's here. The Tigglemans nestled into one of the couches, and Kevin and Jerry remained standing, arms linked, eagerly listening.

"Welcome, everyone," said Claudine. "Yes, tonight is our holiday party, but as you all know, this is also serving as an open house for one very special guest. A few ground rules for interacting with her. Don't. This is specifically directed toward those of you working the party this evening. You are not to engage in any conversation with Zara. If she asks you a question, of course you should be polite and answer it. But that is all. Do not attempt to engage in conversation with her. For my team and those of you who are guests, obviously I want you to be charming and hospitable. I don't want you to be standoffish. But neither do I want you to be overly chatty. Keep the small talk to a minimum. Zara's attention should be on the house. Not us. Part of her interest in Aspen is because she wants anonymity. She wants to be treated like a normal person. So that's what I expect you to do. No questions about her work. No 'Where do you get your songwriting inspiration from?' or 'When you're on tour, how do you manage to do those outfit changes so quickly between songs?' None of that. And under no circumstances should you ask her anything about her personal life or her breakup with Liam."

"We'll treat him like Voldemort," Jules said. "He Who Must Not Be Named."

There was laughter among the group, although it quickly died upon seeing the serious look on Claudine's face.

"And finally, there will absolutely be no photos taken of Zara. To ensure this, I'm going to ask you all to please hand over your phones. Louisa will collect them and lock them away so no one is tempted. I have the code to the Lions' safe. They will be returned to you at the end of the night."

Again the group laughed. Again Claudine's face remained serious. When they realized she meant what she had said, their laughter turned into grumbling protests. Henry spoke up.

"I don't think that's necessary, Claudine."

"And I do," she said. "We should be wrapped by eight o'clock. That's two hours. Surely you can all last that long without checking your social accounts or whatever else you might be doing besides your jobs this evening. If your phone is more important to you than getting the chance to be in the same room as one of the greatest entertainers of our time, then by all means you're free to leave. Go now."

Nobody moved.

"No?"

"*We* don't even have phones," said Captain Tiggleman proudly. Mrs. Tiggleman patted his knee.

Louisa moved through the group, collecting them. Once she had them all in a stack, she stood by Claudine's side.

"What about yours?" Kevin asked. "Aren't you going to turn over your phone?"

"Yeah, what about your phone?" Jerry said.

"I need my phone to monitor Zara's Instagram and see if

she posts about the house and tags us," said Claudine. "That's another goal of this evening. We don't just want her to buy this house; we want her to brag about it. We want her to advertise. So no fawning, no fangirling. Be the charming, smart, successful Calhoun + Calhoun friends and representatives you are. Or, especially if you work for me, as always, fear my wrath."

This time Claudine smiled. This time no one laughed.

Then the doorbell rang, a booming series of chimes.

"That's her!" Claudine said. "She's here. Quick, everyone to your stations. Let's get some piano music, some hors d'oeuvres circulating. Guests, please mingle, act natural. Henry, come stand with me to greet her."

Claudine could feel a growing internal power. Complete control of her destiny was within reach. The life she'd always wanted. The life she deserved.

She took Henry by the hand and led him to the front door.

"How do I look?" she asked him.

"Ready," he said.

That word triggered something. She suddenly felt an appreciation for him that she hadn't felt since . . . possibly ever. He could have said "Gorgeous" or "Beautiful" or "Fantastic" or any other word. Instead, he chose the one that she needed to hear. She was ready. In that moment she was struck by how well he knew her. And by how much she needed him. She had always known how much she needed him as an artist—his talent. She had known that from the very beginning. It was the reason she had been so drawn to him, and the reason they had done what they had. But she never knew until that moment how much she needed him as a person—his love. She had been too hard on him lately. It was the stress of the business. Once tonight was over and they had sold the house to Zara, she would focus more on their relationship. Things would be better between them. They could start fresh. Not leave Aspen for good like he suggested, but maybe go on a vacation. Some time for just the two of them to get reacquainted with each other and work things out.

She put a hand to Henry's cheek and smiled. Then took a deep breath and opened the door.

"Happy holidays," said Steve.

Henry

Of course, Henry thought. That's what this house did. It tainted and destroyed everything it came in contact with. It was worse than a haunted house. A haunted house conjured ghosts and apparitions and specters. This house did one better: it summoned the living. Put you face-to-face with your greatest fear. When the door opened, he saw Claudine's face collapse. Then she quickly recovered.

"Steve," she said. "Out caroling this evening? Where are the rest of the singers?"

"Claude, looking beautiful as ever," he said. Claude. "And, Henry—I heard you were in the hospital, but you look terrific. What a relief. I was thinking on the way over here—what would happen to Calhoun + Calhoun without you? Who would build her houses?"

Henry saw him around town now and then. Aspen was too small to completely avoid someone. But they never spoke to each other. Henry made sure of it. A few times he saw Steve walking down the street and crossed to the other side. It wasn't timidity that caused him to do this. It was fear. He was afraid of what he would do to Steve if he got too close to him. He had discovered the rage within himself and the barbarity he was capable of, and he could never allow that to happen again.

"What are you doing here, Steve?" Claudine asked. "You're letting in a draft."

"I came for the party, of course," Steve said. "I even brought my White Elephant gift."

He held up a large shopping bag with a wrapped box inside. By the way he strained to keep it raised, it was heavy.

The Calhoun + Calhoun holiday party wasn't much of a secret in the Aspen real estate community. Enough employees had cycled in and out of the firm over the years that word had spread about the tradition. But how did he know they were having it at the Lions'? Someone must have told him about Zara. He was there to sabotage the sale of Montague House and steal her as a client. Maybe one of their agents had tipped him off to spite Claudine. Or maybe he'd gotten the information from someone at the airport or at her hotel. In Aspen, there were always a few bucks to be made from leaking the whereabouts of a visiting celebrity. Henry didn't blame whoever told him. And he couldn't even blame the house. He was the one who had built it. If anyone was to blame, it was him. Steve showing up was inevitable. That didn't mean they had to let him in.

"Sorry," Claudine said. "No room at the inn."

As she started to close the door, the headlights of a black SUV pulled in the drive.

"Oh, that must be her," Steve said. "I'll wait. Say hi to Zara. I'm sure she'll ask me why I've been turned away. It'll be awkward, but I'll have to tell her . . . everything."

Steve was right. It *was* too late. If they wanted to sell the house to Zara, they couldn't make a scene. And now Henry *did* want to sell the house to Zara. Up until now he hadn't cared. His career was over tomorrow either way. Steve trying to poach her from Claudine, though, that changed the game. Now he had to protect what was his. Ready to compete. Busting up Steve's plan and securing the Zara sale wouldn't make up for what he had done to them, to their marriage. But at least it was something—a small bit of retribution.

"Come in," Henry said. "Louisa will take your coat and your phone. And Jules will take your gift."

It was only 29 degrees outside, but as they stood on the front step, about to greet Zara, Henry felt a trickle of sweat drip down his back.

PART TWO

The Affair

Claudine

Everything was supposed to change the day she received her real estate license. The previous two weeks had been nothing but constant studying, and the night before the exam she hadn't slept at all. Between working full-time as a receptionist at The Gilman Agency and taking classes, not a moment was wasted. Like most young people in Aspen, after college she had come for the skiing but quickly found working as a sales associate in the pro shops to be too mind-numbing and ambitionless. She answered an ad to pay the bills and find something more challenging. It only took a few months before she realized she had a knack for understanding the ins and outs of real estate. All you really had to do was learn how people worked, and wasn't her sociology degree at least good for that? Besides, it wasn't all bad. She and Steve, her boss, got along, and every Friday the agency hosted a happy hour in the office.

Around the same time she got the receptionist's job, she met Henry. They were both eating alone at the bar of the Red Onion. She was reading the *Aspen Tribune*, an article on the new tourist information booth, and Henry leaned over and said, "I designed that." Later, when she got to know him better, she would think back with surprise at how forward he'd been. That wasn't like him at all. He was shy, humble. It made her realize the kind of effect she'd had on him, that he simply *had* to get her attention. She was genuinely impressed as he explained it was his first gig out of school; a friend of a friend's father needed some quick, cheap labor. Henry tricked the place out without going over budget. Reclaimed wood, rock floors, an air purification system created by a plant wall. His talent and potential were immediately clear to her. Three months later, she was the one who first mentioned marriage. She knew he had a gift and in the right situation could achieve greatness. She could help him get there—help *them* get there. Faster. It always felt like her life wasn't moving fast enough. She wanted more, now. What was so virtuous about patience? That maxim made no sense, especially if you abided by that other one about life being short. She said they should forget a big wedding and go straight down to the county clerk's office on East Main Street. Henry wasn't so sure. Didn't she want a fancy ceremony and a big ring? Yes. Of course. But she knew greater opulence was in store. What mattered most was locking him in. When she knew, she knew. And she wanted him. Assured him that he'd get her a big fat ring in a few years. When he was rich and famous for his designs. "You will be famous," she told Henry. Eventually he did get her a ring: 3.02 karats.

In her opinion, Henry was underused and underappreciated at his job. It was a small but respected commercial design firm that did uninteresting projects. During this crunch time, before her real estate licensing test, Henry was crucial.

Taking care of anything logistical—the bills, the shopping, the cleaning—so she could be laser focused. It was the only time in their relationship when their own house wasn't the picture of order. He was going through a model building phase; she was always looking for a pen. They were young, and the excitement of knowing the next part of life was about to start, that everything was ahead of them, made working that hard easy.

The morning she passed, it was Steve she wanted to see first, not Henry. She couldn't wait to tell him she was ready to be his new star agent. He was on the phone when she burst into his office. Without looking, he shooed her out and continued pitching whoever the sorry sucker was on the other end of the line, his lips smacking like a beast, the saliva in his mouth spraying his desk with each word. Not the reception she was imagining.

Claudine walked back to her desk. All around, agents were happily chatting with potential clients. None of them were her friends, nor had they been particularly nice during the year she had been there. In a bold moment, Claudine had asked Steve why he'd hired half the sales team in the first place. She didn't see what was so special about them. They seemed exactly mediocre.

"That's precisely what's special about them," Steve said.

They worked for him, he needed to make sure they never forgot that. Now, looking at them, she started to understand what he had meant. Truth, some customers like dealing with someone average. They don't ever want to feel threatened. They feel safest doing business with someone bland. These people drive Volvos, watch *Seinfeld* reruns, invest in low-risk mutual funds. Safe players. Patient.

She went back to her desk. There was a package and a card waiting for her. She unwrapped it. A thin white picture frame. She opened the card. *For your license. I'm so proud of you and can't wait to celebrate tonight. Love, Henry.* He was planning on cooking her a celebratory dinner. Finally crack open that bottle of rare Scotch they'd received from his coworkers as a wedding gift.

Steve appeared at her desk. His lame congratulations already felt too late. He was off to Snowmass for an appointment, not even considering the possibility that she might join him, now that she was a licensed agent. It was clear that nothing had changed: she was to answer phones and file paperwork. It was frustrating. It didn't matter that his offer to take her out for a celebratory drink after work was in reaction to the disappointment on her face. It was the opening she needed.

"I'll make us a reservation," she said.

Then he was gone, leaving Claudine to sit and stare at the phone. This wasn't going to work. She had to find a way to stand out. Sifting through a stack of everyone else's purchase and sales agreements, she was quick to realize these were not going to be her clients. Poseurs. Riffraff overextending their credit lines, barely scraping together minimum down payments, needing private mortgage insurance. No, her clients would be different. She stayed in Aspen for one reason: the luxury market, the endless supply of money and the rich's desperate need to spend it. Those were the kind of clients Steve dealt with. Clients like that weird husband and wife, her with the plastic surgery and him wearing that captain's hat. The Tigglemans. If she wanted that business, she would have to learn more than what was on her real estate exam. She would have to learn his secrets and methods. And she would have to give him a reason to teach them to her.

Pushing Henry as far from her thoughts as possible, she picked up the phone and made a reservation at Ajax Tavern. A table in the back, please. Later, after she and Steve had polished off a perfect coq au vin with a bottle of pink champagne, she suggested a nightcap at J-Bar. She knew it was one of his favorite spots. They sat close on leather stools and Steve told her stories until closing. Dry cabernet after dry cabernet, she asked question after question. He was dizzy, drunk on the sound of his own voice. Going on and on about how Aspen had changed over the years and where he saw new opportunity cropping up everywhere. It was like a master class in real estate theory, and there wasn't a bit of information she didn't file away. God, the man loved to talk about himself. She was learning more about the business in one evening than most would in their first few years.

She liked the mystery that came with figuring out what made him so successful. Her analysis was acute. Start on the surface. Perhaps his defining characteristic was that, year-round, his skin was a nice shade of orange. Steve made no secret of the fact he tanned. Actually, he was open about it in the most intriguing way. He normalized it. Got in a good tan today, he'd brag. He was one hundred percent Aspen. Claudine was unable to imagine him in any other environment, any other town. There was no way he could exist walking down the streets of New York—or any city, for that matter. He could exist only here. She had to admire his singular nature, the mixture of gaudy and charm that kept him universally well-liked, which was tough to do in a place of so many economic disparities. There were the rich who owned and the poor who rented, usually down-valley, with hardly anything in between. But it was hard to find a person who didn't like Steve.

No one cared if he showed up to important meetings without a pen. In seconds, five people would be tripping over each other, volunteering to take notes, offering up their own pens. She had been one of them. Claudine cherry picked which of his strategies were of use to her. "Strategies." His word, reflecting his obsession with motivational and self-help books. More like scams. Even more accurate: lies.

Steve was a master of reading a situation and conveniently reciting exactly the right anecdote to seal the deal. Truth played no part in the matter. *If you listen very closely,* he'd say, *you'll start seeing how through simple conversation people reveal so much personal data.* Those details were as valuable as currency—what eventually translated *into* currency. The equation was simple. *A small piece of personal information plus a dash of something magical equals exactly what they want to hear. Think aspirational. Tailor the story to who they want to be rather than who they are.*

When a Houston-based oilman with a bemused look on his face showed up wanting to buy a "shack" to do some fly-fishing in the spring, Steve told him it was his lucky day. Jack Nicholson's old place was on the market. It was right near a sweet spot on the Roaring Fork River. He and Jack pulled nine trout out of the hole one afternoon last July, all over eighteen inches. Cooked them up right there on the riverbank. Jack liked to carry a little satchel of salt in his pocket, which made all the difference. It was the best meal he'd ever had in his life.

That night at J-Bar, after Steve finished telling Claudine that story, he had a good laugh over his tall tale. It had worked. The oilman couldn't sign the papers fast enough. A specific place like the Roaring Fork River. A particular number like nine. A distinct item like the little satchel of salt. The details were what mattered. People wanted to believe. The details were what allowed them to.

But Steve wanted to believe too. He wanted to believe he was attractive. That Claudine desired him. He wasn't immune to deception. Or maybe he was. Maybe he knew what Claudine was doing but thought it was a fair trade-off. Whether he was unwitting or not, Claudine didn't much care. By the time they walked out of the bar and he started to kiss her, she had convinced herself that going down this path would eventually be good for both her and Henry. If enduring a few clumsy encounters lasting less than ten minutes was going to leapfrog years of navigating proper channels and complaining about the daily grind, it was worth it. She was a quick study. Which was why she knew not to let it go further than a kiss that night. She knew the value of what she had. It was a seller's market.

Henry

It was almost one in the morning.

Lying on the couch, Henry repositioned, tucking the blanket tighter around his legs, finding a better spot on the pillow for his head. The TV was on but he was only occasionally watching. Then sleeping. Sleeping. Then drinking. The fabric wet with drool. He flipped it over.

Where the hell was she?

Three hours late.

The champagne long gone, the inverted bottle bobbed in the silver bucket. He killed it quickly after the first hour. He didn't even like champagne, but it went down fast and smooth and at first made waiting a little easier. At this point he still thought she was only late but coming. After all, the celebration was for her. Who missed their own party? Even if it was just the two of them. She worked too much to have any real friends, something he was sure would change at some point. Around the second hour, he pulled down the bottle of Scotch from the back of the liquor cabinet. It was from the smallest distillery in

Scotland. He opened it. She didn't really care for Scotch anyway, complained that it tasted like fire and dirt. That's exactly what he felt like: dirt.

He called the office. No answer. Of course not, it was so late . . . Why hadn't she called?

Another hour of Scotch and watching the old ski flick *Downhill Racer*. The local station played it all the time. It was a favorite of his. He'd stopped skiing after high school, could no longer stomach the scene it had become. But watching Robert Redford conquer the slopes was exactly what he needed to forget he was waiting for her until finally he heard the key turn in the door. Then the clicking of her heels as she walked from the door to the little bench. She was taking off her shoes, probably rubbing the arches on her feet. His drunk confusion turned to slow-motion panic. Where had she been?

The keys must have fallen out of her pocket, because they clattered on the floor. The thought of her anger, that way she could get, made him bury deeper into the couch. Had he done something to make her mad? Want to avoid him? Somehow she could switch around an entire situation with a sigh and make Henry feel like *he* was the one who'd failed *her*. It was one of her best tricks, the one he most feared. It was probably all a misunderstanding. Maybe he'd heard her wrong on the phone. That must be it. He had been wrong. Their celebration was going to be tomorrow night. Sometimes he was not great with details. Henry let his arm fall to his side and his fingers grazed the coolness of the hardwood floor. He patted about. There it was. Expertly, he lifted the Scotch glass to his lips without moving his head and tossed back the last of the Edradour.

There she was. Smiling and shrugging out of her coat, leaving it in a pool on the floor.

"They surprised me at work with a party."

"Why didn't you call?" She was staring at the empty bottle next to the couch.

"Thought we were saving that Scotch."

"Thought we were celebrating your real estate license," he snapped, immediately regretting it. He hadn't meant to.

She let it hang, then softened.

"Let's celebrate this weekend?" she said. "Steve and I have client meetings the next few nights. But let's go to Mezzaluna on Saturday. You and me."

Then she was gone and he heard the water in the shower turn on.

He struggled to sit up. Then to stand. Standing, he found he was drunker than he thought. It took a moment to steady himself. Making his way down the long hall to the bedroom, his arms pulled him along the corridor like the rope tow on the bunny hill. She'd left the bedroom door open and there was a trail of clothes leading to the master bathroom. A belt . . . her skirt . . . the white blouse with ruffled cuffs . . . lacy rose-colored bra . . . The bathroom door was cracked slightly, steam drifting out. Quietly, he shuffled to the door and wedged himself in the frame. Sliding down to the floor so his back was straight, knees bent, feet up against the other side. He closed his eyes; the escaping steam felt good on his face. A faint smell of eucalyptus. He wanted it to go on forever. He would be very, very quiet and she wouldn't even know he was there.

There had been a work celebration.

Everything was fine. Nothing was wrong. Not now, not nestled in his comfortable hiding place with steam on his face and his love right on the other side. Everything was perfect. That was where he woke up the next morning, curled in front of the bathroom door, alone, a blanket on him. Claudine off to work. She must have had to step over him when she was getting ready.

From that night on, she was gone most nights. Client dinners. Late showings.

He went smaller. Drank more. Talked less. Only whiskey made things better. His new nightly routine after work was sketching with a glass of wine, then watching television with a bottle of whiskey, just sinking back into the worry, letting it consume him. Even if he didn't want to admit it, he knew.

She was having an affair, and it was exhausting.

Claudine

Claudine didn't exactly consider it an affair. Or a dalliance, a fling, a tryst, a booty call, a hookup. All of those suggest romance, passion, or just plain lust, and she didn't feel any of that for Steve. This was purely work. A transaction—that's how she saw it.

By her initial estimate, she thought it would take three months to scrub him for what she needed, but after two she felt done. The mentor-mentee-lover relationship cemented, she'd made it to the inner circle quicker than she thought. Now she couldn't wait for it to end. It had gone well. Methodically she'd made sure to meet every contractor he knew, photocopied his lists of past clients and cold-call leads. She had boxes of documents and critical correspondence, and listened in on every call she could. The last part was about learning how to get a listing and she succeeded.

But it was time to be home. Henry needed her, especially with his drinking getting so out of control.

It would be a relief to have it over. Henry didn't know how

close they were to starting their own business. She couldn't wait to tell him. Of course, she couldn't tell him everything. Even if she had convinced herself it was all for the greater good, she didn't have real feelings for Steve. Henry wasn't the type to understand a situation as complicated as this. His drinking had become a problem. She wasn't sure how to handle it, which didn't happen very often. He used to talk about working toward a promotion at the firm; now he wasn't even sketching very much. Going in late a few mornings each week wasn't exactly the path to becoming a partner. It was obvious at some point she was going to have to step in; he wouldn't be able to do it alone.

That morning, when she walked into Steve's office, in her mind it was already done. She'd been growing bolder with each sale. Getting better. The week before, after selling a two-bedroom condo for 10 percent above market, she talked the property manager into introducing her to different owners in another complex he managed who were looking to sell. By the end of the day she picked up three more properties to represent.

Steve was drinking coffee and reading one of his pathetic paperbacks, *Help Yourself to a Better You*, which made him look insignificant.

"Why do you read that?"

"Claude," he said with exasperation, "books like these are read by most of America and all of our industry. Research. Desperate types, searching for an answer. I'm reverse-psychology reading. We must understand the way they think. Does that make sense?"

"Of course that makes sense," she said. "You're speaking English."

He laughed like he always did, chalking up her attitude to youth and ignorance. Mistake. Steve was also a master in underestimating.

"Listen to these chapter titles," he went on. "'Chapter One: Dressing Mutton Up as Lamb. Chapter Two: Be Your Best Self by Being Someone Else. Chapter Three: Eye Contact Is the Key to the Wallet—'"

"Steven, it's all so pedestrian."

"*Steven?*" he laughed. "My mother calls me Steven."

"I just wanted to stop in and say thank you," she said, taking a seat across from him. "I would not be able to do this if it hadn't been for all you taught me."

"What are you talking about?" His eyes narrowed.

"I don't want you to worry. I won't be suing you—"

"Sue me—"

"I just said I *won't be*. Let me explain what's going to happen. First, it's not only over, it never happened. *We* never happened. Second, I'm taking the Tigglemans with me."

"Claudine, what are you doing—"

"I believe chapter four is called 'This Is the Price of Doing Business.'" She lingered, savoring the moment, then politely and pointedly said, "Goodbye."

She needed to find Henry. It was finally time.

Henry

When he got home from work, he could sense a shift immediately. There were candles lit. Fresh flowers in a vase. He smelled garlic, something baking in the oven. The table was elaborately set for two. A record was on.

Was this the right house?

Yes, there was his couch, lately his bed, but the blankets were folded nicely, draped over the back. The pillow gone. Not as he had left it.

"Henry?" Her voice so sweet, it was jarring.

He went to the bar cart and poured a whiskey, his growing collection impressive.

"Henry?" she called again from the kitchen.

He could hear her banging around, the sound of a spoon stirring a pot. A cork coming out of a wine bottle. Then she was in front of him. Dressed up, wearing the emerald drop earrings she bought after making her first sale a few weeks ago, a present to herself. Handing him a glass of wine, she asked him to sit. He had a drink in each hand. She was excited, he could tell. Why was she acting like this was how each day normally ended? He finished his drink and took a sip of wine.

"I have an announcement," she said.

She looked like a memory of someone he used to know. But it was her. It had been so long since they'd even been home at the same time. He didn't expect the swell of emotion that came with her attention.

She did most of the talking. There was big news: she had quit her job. No more late nights. But there was no need to panic. She had a plan. He hadn't noticed the folder on the table. Then she was laying out letterhead, envelopes, notepads, business cards. She handed him one. There were simple hooked *C*'s in the upper corner as a logo.

Henry Calhoun
Architect, Partner
Calhoun + Calhoun

She explained that this was what she'd been working on so late every night. So hard. Wanting to surprise him. Wasn't it perfect? As she made the excuses and said the words, it didn't seem to matter that he knew it wasn't true. Or at least wasn't the whole story. He chose her side of things. To live this version of his life, the one in which he believed everything she said as the truth. *Calhoun + Calhoun.*

She spoke like he was supposed to already have known the plan was in the works, to make him feel as if he'd been included in the idea from the start. That this, the business card he held, was the manifestation of everything they've been dreaming of. She had her eye on a perfect little office smack in the middle of downtown. Lots of windows. Everything white. They'd take out a loan. Modest, for sure, but just what they'd need to launch the business.

"You'll finally work on your own houses. I've been selling more and more. And that can support us until we can start developing. Then, when the timing is right—when we find the perfect plot of land—we'll build. And sell. Repeat."

"Repeat," he repeated.

"Can't you see it?"

She was reminding him of before, not so long ago, when they'd get excited about having adventures, starting careers.

Slowly it was setting in.

She'd come back.

This was their second chance.

Claudine

There's no instant glory when starting a business. Only hard work. The big dream, the vision of helming an immediate well-oiled machine, quickly gives way to realities. To needs. An office. Clients. New clothing. Claudine did a complete wardrobe wipeout. She couldn't fathom, even for a moment, the thought of wearing a skirt she'd been a receptionist in. Building around a few key designer staples would be important. A Chanel tweed dress. An Yves Saint Laurent wool suit jacket. A string of pearls. Gradually she'd add to it. For now, the rest she could pick up at Pitkin County Dry Goods. She started taking yoga and got a new haircut, her long curls chopped into a severe bob. It was edgy, intimidating, powerful. Henry didn't even recognize her at first.

She'd never built something from the ground up, but, through extensive reading and research, knew enough not to be disillusioned when things didn't go exactly the way she'd envisioned. The first thing to go was the idea of a brick-and-mortar office. After looking at two spaces (one on Hyman that had no windows, the other on Hopkins—cute but outrageously overpriced); she decided they didn't need one for the first year. It would be a waste. There was plenty of room in the living room at the condo. Keeping a low overhead made sense. Stay the course. Hardly any agencies in town offered what they did—the complete package. The goal was development. An architect with bold, innovative ideas and a rising real estate star with impeccable taste. A husband-and-wife team. It was a good story. Calhoun + Calhoun would be a tough birth, but worth it.

The immediate need was to find the land. This was boom time, and most people sitting on worthy plots and looking to sell had cashed out. A house bought for under ten thousand dollars in the 1950s was worth millions now. And there were no signs of it slowing down. When land became available, it was getting purchased within a day of being listed, if it got listed at all. And the prices kept going up. Soon they wouldn't be able to afford even a half acre. It only made her work harder. She knew they'd find it; it was only a matter of when.

Ideally it would be a few miles out of town. Something truly spectacular. They had one shot to establish a reputation. The first house would set the tone. Claudine decided that she would keep selling condos and houses—whatever listings she could get—until they found the perfect plot. She'd spend hours driving around Snowmass and Buttermilk. All around Red Mountain and Woody Creek. Not that she expected to find a fire sale, but she thought she'd discover something. The only thing she was learning was that big companies already owned so much. They needed another way in. A connection. She refused to be discouraged. Worked on her patience, which wasn't easy. It would come. She'd find it. And until then she and Henry would gather the troops. Establish a stable of excellent hardworking local vendors. Meet the master masons. Befriend the top wood restorers. Find the best metalworkers.

Claudine knew early relationships with like-minded, ambitious, skilled contractors would be crucial when it became go time. The Alpine brothers were the best custom-home builders in the state. Always in high demand. The good news was Henry already knew them. Third-generation Aspenites, Jack and Bobby—the new generation taking over the business—had been a couple years older than him in high school. The currency that went with Henry's local status got them the meeting, and the partnership was cemented over a dozen beers at Little Annie's. When it did happen, it would happen fast. But they'd be ready. The key was to have a top core team to execute Calhoun + Calhoun houses, and they were on their way. She saw herself as a commodity trader, but instead of dealing with grain or gold, it was luxury, bespoke real estate. Everything new. Everything exciting. Years from now, she wanted Calhoun + Calhoun rolling off the tongue of anyone looking to buy in Aspen. It was during these early days when she learned that starting over came easy to her. She was good at it. Which would soon prove more helpful than she could ever know.

Henry

Maybe it was fitting that it all started with a ghost story.

It was Halloween, and they'd been sitting around the fire-pits outside the Little Nell, having cocktails and trying to scare each other.

"None of us ever saw that kid Danny again," said Henry. "Then Mr. Miller put up about a hundred or so 'No Trespassing' signs. All this only made us more curious. I mean, we were ten. We'd sneak up to his property and hide in the trees. He lived in this shitty cabin and had this crumbling barn. I remember bringing binoculars once. We'd sit there and wait. Wait for something to come out of the barn. I was almost disappointed when we found out the reason we never saw Danny again was because his family moved to Denver." Henry laughed. "But, I tell ya, it is so beautiful up there. Surrounded by the mountains, but up high enough to feel like you're on top of the world."

"Is it a contender?" asked Claudine.

"He's one of those guys that would never sell."

"Never say never."

"Literally the best view I've ever seen."

"Why am I just hearing about it now?"

"Claudine, it's not for sale."

"Everything's for sale."

While Claudine was on the land hunt, he'd never been happier designing a dream home. He knew it made more sense to wait until they found the right property. The location would have an extremely important impact on the final design. But he couldn't help it. Feeding on the energy of a new company, so happy how it had reinvigorated their marriage. He'd never been so in tune with his work. Taking meetings with craftsmen, day trips to check out materials firsthand. A perfect day was spending the better part of an afternoon comparing different rough stones. Every part of his design was considered, from the open floor plan he was constantly adjusting based on flow to the zigzag driveway that would eventually deliver you to the front door. In his gut he knew he was creating something special. They were on the brink of great achievement. He was so close to having the house done on paper; they just needed the land.

Find the land, build the house, sell the house.

As pieces were falling into place, he watched with awe as Claudine fed off the momentum. Tackling each problem with precision and patience. She was someone with a vision, yes, but what made her stand out was that she saw the path to completion. Could grasp the big picture from an early stage and figure out in real time how to get there.

She jumped up. "Let's go."

"Where?"

"To your secret plot of land."

"It's a bit of journey. We'd need to drive ten minutes out of town, then turn off the highway and head up about a mile. And that's just where we park so we're out of sight. The rest is on foot, straight through the forest."

"I'm down for an adventure."

"I'm serious when I say we'd need to be careful. Silent. Around these parts, people are shot for trespassing."

It only made her want to go more. He couldn't think of a real reason not to. He'd only had two drinks, which these days, with the tolerance he had, barely made a difference. There were already flashlights in the car. Why not have some fun?

"Let's go now." She was already twisting her hair up into a ponytail, like that would somehow show him she was serious. He laughed. She won. He glanced down at her strappy high-heeled Steve Madden sandals.

"You'll need to change your shoes."

It was dark as they drove. Quiet in the car the way astronauts are quiet driving to a launch. Electric. A nervousness. The anticipation of discovery, the threat of failure. He pulled into the lookout area and turned off the car, leaving on the headlights so they could see the dense forest in front of them.

After a moment, Henry turned on the flashlight, shut off the car lights, and opened the car door.

"How do we get there?"

"We take that." He pointed to a narrow opening in the trees. "An old game trail. We hike up until we hit the dirt road. Then follow the road to the next bend. There, we'll leave the road and carefully walk to a small patch of trees. We'll hide in the trees and spy on the house."

"I love this."

He shone the flashlight and gestured for her to go first. The light bounced on the dirt ahead as she made her way into the trees. She had refused to change her shoes but was moving fast in heels. He was impressed with her balance and agility. They made it to the aspen grove without incident. She wanted to look everywhere at once: the barn, the view, the house. The lights were on in the cabin and they could see Mr. Miller sitting at the kitchen table. It had been almost twenty years since Henry had seen him, but he looked exactly the way he remembered. Baggy overalls, bald except for one thin silver string swept across his forehead and pasted behind an ear. The old barn was still standing, full of shadows, about twenty yards from the house, an outline in the dark.

The old man stood up from the table and walked to the window. It seemed like he was looking straight at them. There was no way he could possibly see or hear them. They were hidden by the trees, the moon was covered by clouds, and they were half the length of a football field away. Still, they froze and held their breath. Dead October leaves swirled, making a creepy crunchy sound. Like footsteps. Mr. Miller pressed his nose against the glass. Maybe he could see them?

Claudine stepped out from behind the trees.

"What are you doing?" Henry hissed.

"I want to get a better look," she said, taking a few steps toward the cabin.

"Claudine!" Henry said, as loud as he thought he could without attracting Mr. Miller's attention. "This isn't funny."

She continued to walk across the meadow, neither fast nor slow, her movements methodical, determined. Even in the overcast darkness, the beauty of the land was on full display. She marched on, taking it all in.

Henry didn't dare call her again but inched out from the grove.

It looked like the old man might have seen her through the window, because then he was on the porch. He stared out into the meadow, scanning in all directions. Claudine just stood there staring back at him, now maybe thirty yards away. Was his eyesight bad? Could he not see her? Mr. Miller did not call out to her, and Claudine said nothing. After a few more moments the old man went back inside. Claudine turned and walked calmly back to Henry.

He stood paralyzed, waiting for her to reach him. When she did, her eyes were big, her cheeks flushed.

"What the hell was that?" he whispered, his breath uneven. Everyone responds differently to danger, and Henry froze up. But Claudine looked radiant. Exhilarated. Turned on.

"This is it," she said. "This is the place. Our land. We'll build the house here."

Henry started to protest but she put a finger to his lips, unzipped his jeans, and pulled them down to his knees.

PART THREE

The Game

Tommy loved working for Mr. Miller. He loved that land. There really was nothing like it in all of Aspen. It had been in the Miller family for three generations. Big skies, a brutal beauty, a sense of solitude. It was Miller's legacy. A generation ago they had even more land, ran a cattle ranch, but for the last few decades it's been Mr. Miller growing old up there by himself. Hired help coming and going. It was just far enough from town not to feel the impact of the crowds during the first boom. The town was built on silver in the late 1800s, and when it lost its value in 1893, Aspen, well, stopped. For a long time it was over. Can you imagine that now? Sometimes I wonder what would have happened if Hollywood hadn't found us. If we hadn't reinvented ourselves.

I remember my mother talking about being excited when people started coming to town again. When the Aspen Skiing Company expanded. It was a second boom. This time, instead of silver, it was celebrities. Fashion came to Aspen. In came the stores. We all learned words like Prada, Gucci, Dior. Nicholson, Douglas, Costner. Friends I'd known since grade school, if they weren't determined to hate the renaissance they were in the middle of, were now putting on lipstick and sunglasses with their cowboy boots just to walk up Mill Street to Wagner Park.

To anyone who only wanted to live in peace, all that pressure came hard and fast. Tommy would tell me how, *literally as a survival tactic, Mr. Miller had firmly established himself as antiestablishment to scare everyone away until they'd all but forgotten him. He liked the fact that he had a reputation as a recluse. His five acres were big enough that he could forget about the mansions being built far out near the property line in all directions. So he didn't have to bother with too many people.*

Mr. Miller never had any children but took time with his hired hands, got to know them. Fed them. Talked to them. He expected them to be strong and work hard, he was strict, but kind. That's what Tommy said. You had to get to know him. He didn't show it to just everyone. Mr. Miller knew how to instill loyalty and always made sure anyone working for him had what they needed. He was a careful, measured man with large hands. Huge. Covered with calluses. Tommy admired his work ethic and his stubbornness. Admired how he wasn't persuaded by money. How he was the furthest thing from a sellout. He'd tell me all about the people who would sometimes stop in to see if Mr. Miller's land was for sale. Vultures. If you don't care about the money, Mr. Miller told him, you take away their power. Everyone's equal. Of course, he had money—his cabin was sitting on it—so it was easy for him to say.

I'm telling you all this because I want you to be able to hold a picture of them in your mind. Of two hardworking, salt-of-the-earth men. I'd even say they were a couple of the last cowboys.

Zara

Initially I thought it was sweet that Henry and Claudine answered the door together. I could tell it was her, the way she called me "darling," just like on the phone. But there was something strange about Henry's smile, like someone drew it on his face. Now I can see how she was almost overenthusiastic that first moment we met. Compensating for him.

She wasn't what I expected. I don't know what I was thinking, but in my head when the door opened I was expecting Claudine Longet to be standing there. The young, fashionable version of herself, the one who shot Spider. So it took a second for me to see her. The Claudines shared a few traits: thin, dark hair, big doe eyes. But this Claudine was taller, less fragile beauty queen, more domineering sharpshooter.

Oh boy, was she in charge from the start. As we were all saying hellos and I was explaining who Dave was, that he wasn't like a guest but my bodyguard, Pip leapt into action. Now Pip loves nothing more than licking shoes, and she went straight for Claudine's. I swear, I saw literal horror on her face, but not for long because Henry jumped in. He bent right down and lifted her up. Pip went crazy licking his face and I think that's the only time I ever heard Henry laugh. They loved each other at first sight. I've never even had that. It was adorable. Thank god I brought her with me, she's always an excellent judge of character and liked Henry right away, which made *me* like Henry right away. They were instant besties.

I think we were in the parlor when Claudine introduced me to everyone. Long ago I learned to be good with names. A little tip Madonna shared backstage at the VMAs. She was right. It's so helpful when you're asking people to get you stuff. Rashida brought me some champagne; Dave gave my gift to Jules. Then there was Alice and Louisa and Natalie. I thought it was cool it was mostly women that worked at the office. Then John and Kevin and Jerry. Some silent nods from the Alpine brothers, Jack and Bobby, like the Kennedys. I could tell they didn't know what to do with someone like me. They thought they had to be overly polite and use phrases like "Good evening" and "Wonderful to meet you," which didn't exactly roll off their tongues. I appreciated how respectful they were and loved the whole look: big and rugged. Then the Tigglemans. Or—excuse me—Captain and Mrs. Tiggleman. They looked exactly how you'd want them to look—like they just walked off a yacht. I asked him what he was a captain of and he said, "Nothing anymore. Spent forty years on the high seas. Stationed in Norfolk. I've seen it all: breaching blue whales, men going mad, and more than a few pirates."

"When he retired, it was my turn to choose," said Mrs. Tiggleman. "He wanted to stay on the coast, but I've always loved the mountains. In many ways Aspen's like an island. So it was a compromise."

At this point I'd met everyone except the man with the orange face who was inching closer to me by the second.

"This our dear old friend Steve," Claudine finally said.

"I prefer 'old colleague,'" he said. "Zara, I like your spirit. Not scared of house shopping in the middle of the gray wolf reintroduction happening in these parts. Just make sure you keep that little pooch indoors. Those wolves are fierce hunters."

I couldn't tell if he was joking and didn't have time to find out, because Claudine and Henry whisked me away to see the house.

Claudine

The arrival of Steve threatened to throw everything off. Claudine knew sabotage when she saw it. She was determined that his showing up unannounced wasn't going to change a thing and didn't waste any time. Right now, he wasn't the priority.

"Like much of the land around here, this used to be a cattle ranch," she began, leading Zara out of the parlor. "Until they carved the surrounding land into tiny pieces and started building homes. One of the reasons Montague House is so exceptional is the lot size. It just doesn't exist anymore. This much privacy and these sweeping views are unrivaled."

"It's magical," said Zara.

"That's exactly what we liked about the property," added Henry. *Well done, Henry.*

"This was Henry's first house. Our very first project as a company."

"Just like your debut album, *Melancholy Apostle*," he said. "I read an interview you gave to *Rolling Stone* where you said that will always be your favorite record because it was so in-

112

nocent and messy. You said it isn't as polished and complex as your other albums but that's what you love about it. It's the same thing with this house for me. So many things I would do differently now—better, in a technical sense. But I was doing the best I could at the time, and there is beauty and integrity in that which I could never replicate now."

Claudine was impressed. She hadn't thought Henry was taking this night seriously. She never imagined he would have studied up on Zara.

"I forgot I said that," Zara said. "There's a lot of beauty in first ambition."

"Every beam that holds the house up," Claudine said, gesturing as they walked through the rooms, "every window you look out, Henry made it happen. We're not a real estate agency. We're a full-service residential design firm. We're not like Steve whom you just met. He just sells houses. We build homes. It's rare, actually, to be able to meet the architect. And Henry grew up in Aspen, so he brings an invaluable local perspective."

"That's so cool!"

"It *is* cool. Henry, isn't it cool?"

The annoying little dog was at it again, running in circles, trying to get to Claudine's shoes. Her instinct was to kick it. Pip yapped. Why did she bring that fluff ball?

"Should I get John to take your dog? John!" He was by her side in seconds. "Why don't you take it for a treat. There must be something in the kitchen. We're going to show Zara around. Please, take it."

"Pip," said Zara. "Not *it*."

"Of course," said Claudine. "Take Pip."

"Not a problem." John picked the dog up and disappeared.

"Let's start with a quick peek from the deck."

Zara pulled her faux fur coat a little tighter. She looked stunning, perfect for a party around a pool off Mulholland Drive. Not like someone who has any concern for the elements. The black and white vintage Mod go-go dress fit her like skin, complemented by knee-high baby blue leather boots.

They kept underneath the overhang, careful to stay out of the snow and close to the built-in heat lamps. Claudine pointed out the heated outdoor saltwater lap pool, the firepits, the three hot tubs. Explained how each was slightly warmer than the next. She described where the sun rose in the morning and where it set at night. Full southern exposure. Henry was also getting into it, pointing out details of interest. The outdoor kitchen, the outdoor shower lined with roses that bloom late each spring. The built-in freshwater tubs on the lower deck where you could bathe overlooking everything.

"There's nothing like this view," he said. "You can see all four mountains: Aspen Mountain, Aspen Highlands, Buttermilk, and Snowmass."

"For now," Claudine chimed in, "you'll have to imagine. The snow's out in full force to greet you."

"I remember from the pictures. Insane."

Zara watched, mesmerized as the snowflakes dissolved the moment they smashed against the surface of the heated pool. Snow fell on her face as she craned her neck to see how high the massive windows rose. All the way to the top where they peaked.

"Up here a house needs a steep pitched roof," said Henry, "because of all the snow."

"I've never been anywhere like this," she said, brushing off the flakes that were sticking to her coat.

"Let's go back inside," said Claudine. "We want to show you the observatory, the library, study, the three master bedrooms. There's so much more."

"Is there a recording studio?"

"There can be," Henry said. "I think I know the perfect place. Careful of the ice. The deck's heated, but you never know."

Henry offered Zara his arm. She took it. Henry was good with her, Claudine noted. They clicked. Zara responded to his natural warmth and openness, to the sadness just under the surface. Maybe she sensed the new vulnerability, now that he was also riddled with the fresh anxiety of Steve.

Before they went back inside, Henry brushed the snow off Zara's back. Once safe and warm, he helped her out of her coat and handed it to Louisa. They'd been talking about the volcanic rock he'd used to build the steps below the deck that led to the raised garden bed. Claudine was glad he was loosening up. When he talked about the house, he couldn't think about Steve. Couldn't think about what he'd done. Yes, they could manage this.

"Henry, why don't you keep going. I'll make sure we're ready to start the game."

Henry

"Zara," he said. "Would you like to see my favorite room in the entire house?"

"I'd love that."

Reaching over to the stone wall beside her, he casually pushed one of the dark rocks and a door popped open. A secret passage. He was hit with the memory of Claudine calling it juvenile. How he had fought her on it and eventually won, but only when the Lions said their children loved the idea.

"No way!" Zara exclaimed.

"Follow me," he said. "Every house should have a secret room. A place to hide, to be alone."

The door opened onto a hall with plush red-velvet walls. Sconces led the short distance to a rather large domed room with no windows. Smooth padded walls, checkered carpeting, and rows of luxury viewing chairs sat before the large screen, protected by heavy black drapes.

"The screening room," he said, "though it could easily be turned into a recording studio. You could take all the chairs out and this area could be for the musicians, and the projection booth is big enough that you could make that the engineering room. It's already soundproof."

"I don't hate the idea of a secret recording studio," Zara said. "Then I'd never have to leave."

She flopped down in one of the front-row seats to test how comfortable it was.

"I could sleep here," she said, pushing a button on the arm-rest. It reclined as if it had heard her.

Henry sat down in the seat next to her and told her about the original vision. That he'd been inspired by the old screening rooms from the thirties and forties. In the projectionist's room they could do both 35-millimeter and digital. He could tell the Lions had had the sound system updated. Which was good, technology being so much better now than when it was built. They talked about movies for a while, her love of a good biopic, his penchant for old Westerns.

"My agent wants me to get in the acting game," she said.

"Is that something you want to do?"

"Maybe. It would have to be a perfect fit. Lady Gaga was incredible. I'm not sure it gets better than what she did in *A Star Is Born*. Honestly, I'd worry about control. With music, it's all mine. My ideas, my direction, my handpicked producers. I'm not sure I can trust a form that I don't execute myself."

"Understandable. I feel exactly the same about my work. I'm grateful I found my collaborators early. Jack and Bobby are the best in town."

He was impressed by how articulate she was about her music. Also a bit ashamed that he'd never given her a chance in his mind to be an artist. Assumed there were boardrooms of people writing her songs, styling her, curating every part of her public persona. But no, she was smart. Talented.

"Seems like you know what you want," he said.

"Yeah, I do." She hesitated, then went on. "But I also want to keep changing, you know? I don't like the idea that people will expect me to keep doing the same thing. That's not interesting. Fifty years from now, I don't want to be the Eagles still playing 'Hotel California.'"

"You won't be."

"Thanks. I hope not."

He reclined his seat slightly and pointed up.

"My very favorite part of this room is the ceiling. How the wooden beams are bent like the shell of an arc. All coming together, meeting at the very top. Jack and Bobby Alpine helped me install them. They're all from the same tree; it was fifty feet around."

"Imagine that," she said in awe.

"Extraordinary find. In its prime, a monster of the forest."

A monster. Like him. That's what he wanted to say. He didn't tell Zara this secret room held another secret. Twenty-five feet above, at the very point of the beams' convergence, was where he'd carved his initials. *H.C.* He traced the letters now on the back of his own hand, wishing there were blades on his finger so it hurt, cut, burned—anything to punish him.

Zara

The secret room sold me on the house. So did my conversation with Henry. Like I said before, working with my TM guru had helped me tap into auras, and, honestly, there was something so damaged about Henry. I could sense that he'd taken that—whatever his trauma was—and funneled it into the house, tried to create something good and beautiful that he was missing in his life. Walking out of the secret room, I was ready to sign the contract. We could have done the deal right then and ended the party, but I was looking forward to the White Elephant game and decided to wait until after that was over.

When we got back to the party, everyone was trying to sneak looks at me without being obvious. Which made it all obvious. When you go to enough parties, pretty soon everyone starts seeming like extras. Hired to be there. Actors on a lot dressed for an Aspen Holiday Party, a fractured fakeness. Thankfully, I'm used to it. It didn't take long before I was pretty sure I had everyone sized up pretty accurately. No huge crazies. Everyone who worked for Calhoun + Calhoun seemed very "regular," very "normal." They were all in charge of something. Lighting a candle, straightening the presents, stoking the fire. The whole crew seemed scared shitless even then if you ask me. But I did appreciate that they treated me like I had a brain. By this point, the few conversations I'd had weren't about the music industry but about the history of the area. I even had what was almost a deep conversation with Kevin and Jerry about the holidays in general. What a strange time of year it can be. But also how you're supposed to be happy all the time when in reality it just makes you miss all the things you don't have anymore. It was actually nice. Some people automatically think I'm an idiot. Which gets old.

Then John approached me. We hadn't really spoken yet, but I know the type. Overconfident. Clearly he thought he was sexy, because his eye contact was off the hook. Too much. This is why I started calling him Intense John. I wouldn't say he loved it, but I told him he should feel pretty good; not everyone gets a nickname.

He was like, "Care for any party favors?" Hysterical. What a dork. I couldn't resist fucking with him a little. I asked if he had any blow. It was like springtime on his face, flowers blooming, rainbows coming out of his eyes. Just thrilled. He dropped his voice and said, "Why, yes. I have lots of cocaine in my pocket." I had to tell him to calm down, I didn't do drugs, but Pip did. Could he cut her a couple lines down on the floor?

He was like, "Yes! Of course!"

"Fuck off, Intense John," I said, but nicely. "Pip doesn't do blow either." Then Pip was barking at him; she's the best. He said something ridiculous like "Okay, great!" and walked away. Probably to go freak out somewhere.

The bartender overheard the whole thing and laughed. It gave me a little charge. It was a deep laugh, but he stopped himself when he noticed I was paying attention, becoming professional, but I could see traces of a cat grin on his perfect lips. I like the way his hair was disheveled but his shirt was ironed. Cute. Confident. What was this? I was racing toward heartbreak recovery faster than anticipated. I accepted a glass of champagne from him and was about to say something clever—I'm not above some light flirting—but that was when Claudine announced the White Elephant was about to start.

Claudine

Tapping the side of a champagne flute with a cocktail fork to rouse the attention of a room brought Claudine immense pleasure. She was an expert. Knowing where to place her fingers on the glass, the exact part of the flute to strike, the right amount of champagne necessary to achieve the desired pitch, the right part of the fork to create the perfect ring. Strong and clear. The note sharp enough that everyone stopped talking and turned to find her.

"It's White Elephant time. Fill up your drinks and please find a seat. There are a variety of savory bites and hope you brought your sweet tooth. There will be macaroons, mousse pots, classic candy canes. And much more."

After a brief rush to the bar, anticipatory chatter at full blast, the guests made their way into the living room. Welcomed by the smoky scent of burning apple wood in the air. The Tigglemans practically trotting. The last time they moved that fast was to find the heat lamps at the Aspen World Snow Polo Championship. They might be old, but they were enthusiastic White Elephant novices.

The room was inviting. Two long leather couches, three deep navy armchairs with foot stools, the white chair by the fire, and two mid-century benches. They were arranged in a wide semicircle so guests could enjoy the fire as well as watch the snow fall through the windows. A smattering of small side tables and chic wooden coffee tables for drinks. A white shag carpet in the center. Steve was talking close with John, Rashida, and Jules, then they were all laughing at something he was saying. It was unacceptable that they would even speak to him, let alone encourage him with laughter. He wasn't even funny. The suggested intimacy made her think one of them invited him. No. She wouldn't be distracted in this way. Watching him play the flitty guest, buzzing his way around her party. Apart from Steve, things were as they should be. The conversations light, the guests tipsy, a good moment to start the main event.

"I've saved you the best seat," she said, leading Zara to the white corduroy wingback near the fire. The chair was wide enough for Pip to curl up next to her.

"Great," said Zara, the blush from her champagne showing in her cheeks. Claudine gave the piano player a nod and he began playing "Baby, It's Cold Outside." Claudine had chosen each song personally, looking to tap into the very special holiday spirit. Involuntarily Zara began to hum along. This was almost too easy. Everyone took seats.

Of course Jules conveniently saved a place next to her for Henry. Fine. Claudine was about to take the seat on the bench next to Zara, when Steve jumped on it. He was becoming more impossible by the minute.

"Darling, we're *starting*," she called across the room to Henry. He stood and came dutifully by her side.

"As tradition dictates," Claudine explained, "we'll begin by reading the poem. Some people have taken to calling this game Yankee Swap. That would indicate it has origins in America. However, the pastime can be traced all the way back to this translated Danish poem from 1857 where it was referred to as a White Elephant. It pre-dates even Aspen."

This was a complete lie. Claudine had written the poem herself. But as Steve had taught her, people wanted to believe, and the details were what mattered.

She took the old, yellowed envelope from the mantel, opened the flap with great care, slid out the card, and read:

Say now, young friend, it's holiday time!
With snow and gifts and cheese and wine.
The night you wait for with all your heart
When at last the White Elephant game will start.

What awaits you wrapped tightly in ribbons and bows?
Mystery, excitement, and likely some woes.
The game is designed to expose your true nature
It is not for those afraid of a little danger.

Go forth, be bold, take the gift that speaks to you
Even steal from your neighbor if you want to.
Be nasty, not nice, take what you like best
Now is the time to put your treachery to the test.

Begin.

The ritual over, Henry returned to his seat and from the mantel Claudine took the Tiffany rock-cut bowl containing the numbers Jules had so delicately written. Of course she'd removed her own to secure her spot, and the one for Zara was expertly palmed in one hand. She began pacing in front of the fire.

"There are fifteen of us tonight," she said.

"Sixteen," corrected Steve.

"Every piece of paper in here," she ignored him, holding up the bowl like an offering, "holds a key to the game. Your key. Each has a number. The choosing will be random. Stay where you are; I'll come to you. Remember, this is the only time in your life that you don't want to be number one. It leaves you open for the first steal."

"How many times can you steal?" asked Zara.

"Once per round."

"Is that right?" asked Rashida. "I feel like we debate this every year."

"And every year it's the same answer," said Claudine. "For example, if Rashida steals a gift from Alice, Alice can't just steal it back. She must choose from the table. Your number is your number. No switching, no peaking, no cheating. We'll go in order. Select a gift from the table, bring it back, and open it in front of the group. Let the games begin."

Claudine did as she said, stopping before each guest with the bowl. Holding eye contact with them as they dipped their hand in, making the selection. It was another moment she liked. The locked gaze. Like the poem, it brought some extra drama. Raised the stakes and made everyone feel they were part of something important. Which, of course, they were.

When she reached Steve her eyes went cold. His twinkled as he picked his number. He'd never been able to hide his motives, whether it was a grope in bed or, like now, challenging her openly without saying a word. Telling her not to feel safe. He'd come for a reason and she'd better be on guard. There wasn't a chance she'd react to his silent threats, and she moved on as quickly as she could.

By the time she reached Zara, she slyly let the slip of paper that had been cupped in her palm slide down into the bowl, careful no one saw. She wasn't quite as stealthy as she thought and Zara caught it, giving her a quizzical look. But Claudine could tell she approved.

"Your turn." Claudine smiled. Zara opened it to find the best number of all. The coveted finale, sixteen. She'd have her pick of the lot. The empty bowl went back on the mantel and Claudine gave Steve a look that said, scoot over. He obliged and made room for her on the bench. She took her seat next to Zara. Annoyingly, Pip gave a small growl. Making peace with the beast was a necessary move. She leaned down to its ugly little face until they were nose to nose and whispered just loud enough for Zara to hear, "Pip-kins, you ready for the game?"

"Wait!" said Zara. Whipping out her phone, she expertly positioned herself in frame as she propped Pip under one arm. The fire blazed behind them. "Quick selfie."

Snap, snap.

"What's your handle?" she asked.

"At Calhoun and Calhoun," Claudine and Louisa said at the same time.

Tap, tap, tap.

"Oh," said Zara. "I have zero service."

"That's not usually the case," said Claudine.

"It must be the weather," added Jules.

"That's okay," said Zara. "I shouldn't have even tried. I love how no one's on their phones in Aspen. So present!"

Not a setback; Claudine was confident she could get Zara to post later. For the moment she'd take pride in knowing collecting the phones set the right tone. And, now, it was time to start.

"Who's the sorry soul that's been blessed with number one?"

My father started whittling as a kid, could carve anything. Moving on to clay he'd take from the mountains. Soon he was making casts, teaching himself to heat metals and pour molds. You know the statue, the one on the dresser? He made that. It was the first one he was truly proud of. Worked endlessly to get the details perfect. The cowboy on the horse with the gun. His back arm raised so his aim was straight. Locked and loaded. The horse magnificent, with only the slightest hint of fear in its eye, though he held his head high in mid-stride. A true work of art.

He gave it to me when I was a young girl. And I gave it to Tommy. His room in Mr. Miller's house had nothing. A bed, a dresser, that's it. I was trying to help fill the space. Brighten it up. The whole house was pretty barren. I wanted Tommy to feel like it was his home too. Tommy loved it, said he knew exactly where it would go. Of course I thought it would be in his room—but the next time I was there I was surprised to find it on the mantel. When Tommy had come home that day, Mr. Miller complimented the statue and Tommy ended up offering to put it in the main room so they could both enjoy it.

The two of them had a sweet relationship. The old man was harmless, just the type who wanted to be alone. Not a cruel bone in him. And yes, Tommy could flare up, had a temper, but his deep kindness always won out. No way was he capable of doing what the police said.

Zara

I was impressed but not surprised that Claudine made sure I got the best number. I didn't think she played like that, since up until that point she'd been so serious and earnest about the White Elephant. Her focus had been all business trying to sell the house to me. Initially she let very little of her true self show. It was fun to find out she was a little bit bad. A little bit. Ha! That's the understatement of the century.

By the time we started the game, Pip had made her way back to Henry. Snuggled on his lap. All night she was going back and forth between us.

Cookies had been set out on towering trays like an English tea party. Macaroons, my favorite. Between that and Henry's comments about the *Rolling Stone* interview, clearly everyone had done their homework. I like the salted caramel ones best. How they melt in your mouth. You don't have to chew too much. They just . . . dissolve. Delish. I ate four and slipped Pip one.

Jack Alpine was number one. He walked to the table and circled it, surveying the presents from every side. He chose a box wrapped in leather with an embossed bow burned on the top.

"This looks good," he said. He had some trouble opening it. The snaps were so little. Definitely his hands would be more comfortable around like an axe. It was like a live-action unboxing video—my second biggest YouTube obsession after clips of Claudine Longet singing on Andy Williams's old variety show. Inside was a small glass case. He lifted the top off and looked baffled. He glanced at his brother, who shrugged.

"It's the Gucci belt buckle!" cried Mrs. Tiggleman. It was totally obvious Mrs. Tiggleman had brought it. I'm going to guess she'd never looked more alive.

"Don't worry, Zara," Claudine said. "Aspen has a Gucci store on Galena." This was actually good to know.

Alice was number two. Immediately she took the belt buckle from Jack. People shrieked like she'd stolen his car or something. This was fun. Even I was getting into it.

So this meant Jack went again. Back to the table. He took another present. This one much larger, something unmistakably not jewelry, wrapped in crisp, bright red paper. It opened much easier. It was a strange device-type thing. He lifted it from the box and held it up so everyone could see.

"Authentic solid gold nautical compass!" shouted Captain Tiggleman. So far, everyone was really bad at concealing what they brought.

Steve was like, real gold?

And he said, "Real as a heart attack." Then Mrs. Tiggleman elbowed him in the side and shot an apologetic look toward

Henry. To which Claudine threw in a casual, "Don't worry, it wasn't a heart attack."

"I love it," Jack said, wrapping it in his arms. "If everyone could just forget it exists, please."

Third was Mrs. Tiggleman. She was passive-aggressively complaining about how low her number was but still amped up at the same time. Claudine took this as a teaching moment, to remind everyone that there was always a chance they could go again later in the game if someone stole their gift. The beauty of the rules. A game with a second chance. Possibly.

Mrs. Tiggleman went straight for the biggest box on the gift table. Not a shock. It was three feet tall and two feet wide. Simple green paper and a traditional red ribbon tied around its center. The present was almost as tall as she was. She picked it up, happy to find it was light, and slowly wobbled back to her seat. It wasn't until this point that I clocked the flirting between Henry and Jules. She kept finding reasons to touch his knee. It seemed like one-sided flirting, which is always awkward. Then Claudine broke it up by sharply asking him to help Mrs. Tiggleman back to her seat. The tone of her voice wasn't cool, but it looked like he was used to it by how fast he jumped up.

"Nonsense," Mrs. Tiggleman said. She was already there, her small hands moving fast, tearing at the paper with clawlike fingernails. The box was open in no time . . . only to reveal another box. She opened that box only to reveal another box. I joked to Henry that this must be the gift he brought, what with his penchant for hidden rooms and secret passages. Finally, in the fourth box, Mrs. Tiggleman found a long envelope. It was a little much. She opened the envelope, and it was a gift certificate. She gasped like she had just found out she had a secret twin or something.

"No. It can't be," she said. "Is this real?"

People were chanting, "Tell us, tell us."

"The Sanctuary package from the Remède Spa," marveled Mrs. Tiggleman. It was obvious she's the kind of person always on the hunt for the latest treatments or procedures.

"It includes a cutting-edge new peel," Intense John said like he was some sort of peel expert. Mrs. Tiggleman loved it and Captain Tiggleman told her she didn't look a day over forty, then fed her a crab cake. I bet they feed each other at home all the time.

It was Henry's turn next. He chose a small dark green box wrapped with a single white ribbon. You could tell he didn't like being the center of attention, he opened it quickly. Inside was a black velvet pouch; a pair of silver dice slid out.

"These are nice," he said, holding one up so everyone could see. "Aspen silver?"

"That would be my guess," said Rashida. "Not that I would know."

Next, Bobby Alpine, who looked exactly like his brother but slightly younger. He didn't waste any time and stole the dice from Henry. "They'll be perfect for downtime on the construction site," he joked. Henry selected again from the table and from his initial reaction it seemed he hit the jackpot.

"Well, look at this." He almost looked happy. "A full day of fly-fishing with a guide on the Roaring Fork."

Bobby offered to trade back the dice and Henry was like, no way. But then Steve proudly said it was with one of the best local guides. That's when Henry handed it over to Bobby and took back the dice. I'm not sure that was legal, but no one objected. It was amazing how much I was learning about the relationships between these people. I'd had the sense that there was some drama between Steve and Henry. This confirmed it. However, I figured it was a business deal gone wrong or something. It didn't occur to me at that time that Claudine had had an affair with Steve. He was so gross and obvious, and Henry was so handsome and sweet.

Next, Louisa hopped up, grabbed a gift from the table, and opened this beautiful tapestry. I kept waiting for someone to explain its origin. Then, from the corner of the room, Dave of all people said, "That looks Portuguese." He looked embarrassed after he said it, like he'd meant to think it. He nodded to me apologetically and resumed a stoic pose against the wall. No one confirmed or denied if it was Portuguese. They were getting a little better, because I had no clue who brought it.

It's worth mentioning that Claudine had been collecting all the wrappings as soon as anyone opened a gift. But just as she was about to pick this one up, Pip grabbed it playfully with her mouth. They had a little tug-of-war, which Pip loved, Claudine not so much, and after an aggressive tug, Claudine won out. It was weird, but I cut her a break. What was I going to do, tell her to be nicer to my dog? After all, she'd pulled the night together at a moment's notice at my request. And it really was lovely. But there was something that told me not to relax.

It might seem strange to say, but now that I have a little distance, sometimes I like to rethink the night from Claudine's point of view.

It's insane.

Can you imagine being her? Not knowing that you were

minutes away from the chaos that came after? Thinking you're safe from the truth, only to have it all come out like it did? It's sad, not romantic. Not like Claudine and Spider. At least that Claudine knew exactly what she was doing the entire time. Expected the police to come. Called them herself. Knew she'd have to face up. Endure a public trial. I mean, I know she wasn't thinking about that when she pulled the trigger killing Spider cold, but it couldn't have been too far from her mind. She wasn't stupid. The two Claudines were very different.

My attention was drifting; I was ready for the game to move a little faster.

"Who's lucky number seven?" asked Claudine.

That's when Natalie stood and walked to the table.

Henry

He couldn't stop staring at Steve. It had been years since he had had the chance to look at his face this close up. It looked like an old softball mitt. He was older. Good. There was a frailness that even his bravado couldn't mask. Also good. His jealousy didn't surprise him, but the tiny splash of compassion for his old competition did. Sometimes he couldn't blame him for falling for Claudine. She was irresistible, especially then. She was just like Aspen: beautiful on the surface but dangerous underneath. Steve felt his stare and he quickly looked away. The compassion didn't last long, replaced by a sick feeling in his stomach.

Sometimes he wondered what would have happened if he'd never brought Claudine up to see the property in the first place. If they would have built their first house on the bend of a river. Or in the middle of a meadow. A lesser plot. Everything about their lives could have been different. Would he have stopped drinking? He'd never thought about it like that. Would there have been another incident that made him stop? The drinks were coming so fast and frequent then, it's hard to imagine that he'd come to the conclusion it had to end on his own.

Natalie chose a large rectangle-shaped gift. It seemed a little plainer than the rest. No bow. She walked slowly with it, it had some heft. A theme of the night, she, too, was having a tough time opening it. The professional wrap jobs meant they were harder to open: way more tape. Henry was about to help her so Claudine wouldn't snap at him again, but Bobby was closer and offered his Leatherman. She gratefully accepted. Slicing through the cardboard, she hit a wall of Styrofoam. It made a sharp, high squeak as the blade cut into it. Natalie got the top open and gave the Styrofoam a tug. It scraped the sides of the box as she pulled it out, bits of Styrofoam littering the floor. She split open the covering and, using both hands, lifted out a statue. Deep bronze in color, it stood around ten inches tall. A cowboy on a horse, a rifle raised to eye level, his face fiercely concentrating on the target.

"The Lone Ranger?" Rashida joked.

A small sound escaped Claudine, one Henry had never heard before. The glass of red wine slipped from her hand, crashing to the floor, and quickly started spreading toward the white shag rug.

PART FOUR

The Murders

Claudine

The discovery of the land changed everything for Claudine. Over the next few months, she would drive up to see Mr. Miller every week. At first she'd bring small gifts: little pots of local honey, homemade marshmallows dipped in chocolate, sachets of dried rosemary. She didn't expect him to be nice. The picture Henry had painted was of an evil old man toiling away on a mountain. That wasn't the case at all. He was shy. Would say no, thank you, but take her offerings and close the door. Politely.

Then one day Mr. Miller didn't answer the door. Instead it was a young man.

"You're wasting your time," he said in greeting.

"Why, hello," she said. "And who are you?"

"No. Who are you?" His look and attitude said it all. She wasn't welcome. "Nothing here's for sale. You need to leave. The next time you come up here, I'll have to call the police. Consider yourself warned."

This didn't deter her. It motivated her. Made her work

harder. She ditched her office attire of heels, fitted blazers, and cigarette pants for wellies and T-shirts and jeans. An attempt to seem more rugged, more like them. She brought more gifts. Better ones. Fancy smoked salmon, small-batch gin, an antique cribbage board. But the other man's reaction was always the same.

Get off the land.

Stop coming here.

I'll call the police.

One afternoon, carrying a batch of freshly baked chocolate chip cookies in an antique silver tin, she knocked on the door. A sharp whistle pierced the air from behind, making her jump. Turning around, she was face-to-face with the young man, who by this point she'd deduced worked and lived there.

"You startled me." She laughed. "Is Mr. Miller around? I have some delicious cookies I was wanting to drop off—"

"This is the last time you come here," he said. Each time they'd interacted, he'd grown bolder. Got closer. If someone hosed him off and bought him a suit, he wouldn't be that bad. Strong, tall, cloudy eyes that could pass for sexy. The shotgun was at his side, his dirty fingers wrapped around the barrel. He smelled like a cow. A stench of dirt, shit, and death. "He's not interested in selling. What don't you understand?"

"Oh, stop. Who doesn't need an itty-bitty sweet treat now and then. It's really no bother."

"You're not hearing me," he said, taking another step closer.

"I've also brought some brochures for him to look at. Retirement options. Beautiful places, really."

"You need to vacate immediately."

She popped the top off the tin.

"Chocolate chip cookie?" she offered. "Mr. Miller can tell me himself if he doesn't want to see me. We've been having some real nice chats and I know he doesn't get many visitors. Must get lonely up here."

The young man had raised the shotgun so it rested on his shoulder, a threat she didn't plan on acknowledging.

"Tell you what. I'll just leave the cookies on the porch."

She wished him a nice day and was walking back to the car when the sound of the shot scorched her ears. Falling from the sky were pieces of the silver tin and bits of chocolate chip cookie. The bastard had blown up her offering like a clay pigeon.

Henry

Claudine had turned the dining room into a war room: prop-erty deeds and boundary outlines, weather forecasts and fabric swatches covered the table. She never thought for a moment they wouldn't get it.

If Bill Gates and Paul Allen could work out of a garage, they could work from home. Keeping a low overhead was fine with Henry; they ran off Claudine's start-up energy, coffee, and hard-boiled eggs. (She wasn't much of a cook.) Whatever way she wanted it was fine; he wasn't interested in running a busi-ness the way she was. Would rather focus on actual work. Cre-ating the perfect house. A home.

The only hitch was Henry's drinking. It hadn't slowed down. It wasn't so much a habit but an addiction.

Yes, the affair was over. But they'd never once spoken of it. His choice as much as hers. It was better that they dove straight into this next stage in their lives. Calhoun + Calhoun. Still, Steve was never far from his thoughts. Living in a city of less than seven thousand usually meant running into everyone all the time. There were only slightly lower odds during high seasons when the population swelled to around twenty-five thousand. But if you really wanted to, you could make sure it didn't happen. And he really wanted to. Henry managed to avoid Steve. There was no way he was going to subject himself to that level of shame. Feel like he was nothing. A talentless hack with an adulterous wife. The welcome numbing that came with each drink smothered the rage that built up whenever he thought about it for too long.

He knew Claudine had been going to see Jonathan Miller too much. She was convinced she could get him to come around. The plan was to show him that at his age—he had to be in his late eighties—the property was more a burden than anything else. Didn't a nice condo with all the amenities sound like the perfect way to finish out his years? Sell the land and buy the comfort.

For the most part, he viewed her quest as a pet obsession. Something that would pass. She didn't understand these sort of people. They didn't care about comfort or money. It wasn't realistic to think she could talk someone who had lived his entire life in that cabin, on that land, into giving it up. Even if she used all her powers of persuasion, which were plentiful. Henry kept hoping she'd find another spot on one of her epic drives. Everything on his end was coming together, and he was eager to make the final adjustments based on location. He wasn't going to fight her on it, but he didn't want her to feel like a failure. It was Mr. Miller's stubbornness, not her lack of skills.

"I think he just likes his cabin, Claudine."

"Not everyone likes everything to remain exactly the same— every day, day in, day out. Not all people are like you. You keep working on the designs. I'll get the property."

Lately she'd been slipping insults in with normal conversation. Just that morning he'd gotten up a half hour after she did and got a "You certainly slept well." He pretended like he didn't hear her. Wine, whiskey, vodka. It hardly mattered anymore. It tasted all the better on the heels of one of her stingers. Her fixation was morphing her into someone he barely recognized. She'd exhausted every idea. Each time the hired hand shooed her off the property, the verbal assaults took off. This became his favorite time. He loved when she'd start insulting him more directly, more harshly. It was like handing him a free pass to start drinking no matter what time of day it was.

Most times, he wedged himself in the built-in breakfast nook beside the kitchen, where he liked to work on sketches of the house. Claudine expected them soon, and usually by the third or fourth or seventh drink he was enjoying it. Having forgotten his inadequacies, he could get lost in the possibility of a high arch of an entrance or the curve of a banister at the bottom of a wide staircase. Through his work he was discovering a lot about himself. How flow was important to him. Getting from here to there. From one room to the next. He spent hours building solid philosophies behind each choice, not caring if the reasoning was apparent only to him. The very thought was a reminder that there was an art to it all. It wasn't all bullshit. It was how he made sense of the world. He'd sit for hours contemplating what it meant to be deliberate versus instinctual, respecting that they each had their place, especially in relationship to design.

Even though he was back sleeping in their bed, some nights he'd pass out in the breakfast nook. He knew he was drinking too much. It wasn't good. For them as well as for his work. It was starting to feel like he was waiting around for Claudine to get sick of him. For her to say something. He couldn't shake the disappointment in himself. And yet, during this time, amid all the insults she'd thrown his way, she never called him a drunk. She never said he should slow down or take a night off from drinking. Not once did she scold him about the booze. Other things, yes, but about that she let him be. He never understood why, not until many years later, until the night of his death.

Claudine

The night of the murders had been very confusing.

She was sobbing when she burst through the door. Henry sat, drinking his fourth Manhattan at the dining room table, drafting. He looked up and dropped his pencil. Her face was bloody. Her right eye a theatrical mix of pinks and reds.

"Oh my god. What happened?"

"*Jonathan Miller happened,*" she spat. It was crucial she explain it all exactly right. "I've been working hard, so hard, to make this happen. For *us*. For *him*, even. Trying to get him to understand what a *better life* he would have if he sold the land."

"I know you have," he said, focusing on her face. She knew it was swelling up before his eyes. She could feel it. The side of her head was bleeding. Snot dripped from her nose. She found a tissue and blew it noisily. Taking another, she blotted near the wound.

Henry downed the last half of his glass. He dug an ice cube out and tried to press it against her head, but she pushed his hand away. Her breaths were quick and sharp. Attempts to regain control. Her balance was off. Wait: Which one of them was swaying? She could do this. Get through it. The only thing to do was to catch her breath and go on.

"I pulled up and parked in front. Like I've done all the times before. Got out of my car. Expecting to be greeted; I thought, 'He must be excited to have finally made a decision.' Then I knocked. And he answered. The young worker wasn't there. Initially I had a good feeling."

She started to cry harder. This must all be so upsetting for Henry; she never cried. When he reached out to touch her, she shrank back again.

"I'm sorry," she said.

She sank to the floor, her back against the couch, unable to talk. Lightly touching her head in many places, seeking out other injuries, making sure she hadn't missed anything. She needed her space. He sat on the floor too. Nearby, not speaking. Patiently waiting for her to find the courage to continue. Minutes passed before she found her voice. She wanted to be careful to explain each moment. Henry, listening with a glassy-eyed intensity, took a drink from the bottle.

"He looked different . . ."

She stopped. Another tissue. Another nose blow.

"I thought he was going to say, 'I've thought about it, I'm in! Sorry it took so long.' But he was staring at the floor, and when he looked up he called me a bitch and hit me across the face." She turned her cheek so he could see it better. "Is there a handprint?"

He moved closer, bobbing slightly, the whiskey smell prominent. Taking a tissue, this time she let him gently press it against her temple.

"No handprint. Then what happened?"

"He went to hit me again, and I crashed into the wall. It was terrible; my mouth . . . my mouth was screaming . . ."

He hadn't blinked in what felt like ages.

"This is all my fault. You were right. I should've let it go . . ."

He took another swig straight from the bottle. "That motherfucker. Motherfucker. Motherfucker, motherfucker, motherfucker."

"So I ran." The tears were streaming down her cheeks. "I barely got out the door. I pushed him and ran. Faster than I've run in my life. I didn't look back. Got in the car. Turned the engine on. Came straight home." She was shivering.

His face twitched. He was rubbing his hands like he was trying to make fire. Then let out a yell that filled the room.

"I'm calling the police," he said.

"No, we can't. I thought about it. No. Please. The police would side with him. He could say I'd been trespassing on his property and that he told me plenty of times to stay away. And if this were to become a scandal, our company would be finished before we even started. You know the kind of big-money clients we're after don't want to be associated with this kind of drama."

"Then I'm going over," Henry said. "He's not getting away with this."

He tried to stand up but lost his balance and fell back to the floor. It took him a few seconds to finally get up. This was how it usually was for him at this time of night. Why sometimes he slept in the kitchen. Once he was on his feet, he grabbed his car keys.

"No, Henry," she said. "You can't drive. The last thing I need is for you to kill yourself in a car crash."

"Then fuck it, I'll walk."

"Don't be ridiculous. It would take you hours. Please. Just stay here with me. Just let it go. We'll find another property."

"Claudine, one way or another, I am going over there tonight."

She could tell he meant it.

"Fine," she said. "I'll drive you. But I'm staying in the car. I don't ever want to see that man again. Ever."

"You won't have to," he said, grabbing the bottle and heading out the door.

Henry

He woke up having zero memory of climbing into bed the night before, but he was in bed. He smacked his lips. Cotton mouth. A familiar buzzing sound. The thankfulness he was flooded with when he saw the light blues of the duvet allowed him to sink in a little lower. His cocoon. The comforting cool of the pillowcase on his cheek. He turned to see if Claudine was lying beside him.

She was not.

Dragging himself from bed, he made his way to the kitchen. She was leaning against the sink, the newspaper open and covering her face.

"Morning," he said in a gravelly voice. "Any coffee?"

She put the newspaper down and that's when he saw it. Her face. The dried blood. The swelling. The black-and-blue eye. Her eyes were red. She had been clutching the paper, not reading it. Holding it tight. His mouth opened, but he had no voice. Nothing came out. She said his name. Or something that sounded like his name. Dread spread throughout him as he floated toward her. She laid the paper on the counter. A picture of Jonathan Miller. The headline:

ASPEN LOCAL SLAIN IN DOUBLE HOMICIDE

Longtime Aspen resident Jonathan Miller and Thomas James Cooke, who is believed to have been working for Mr. Miller, were found dead on the property early evening. The homicide investigation is ongoing. At this time, no further information is available, but the Aspen Police Department Tip Line is open if you have any information regarding the crime.

It wasn't possible.

His thoughts raced, he was trying to remember.

They'd been driving?

Wait, before that . . . yes . . . Claudine coming home. So upset. Hurt. He'd hurt her. Miller. It was coming back in flashes. He had been in the passenger seat, Claudine driving. Yes, that was right. Up to the house. Yelling who in the fuck did Jonathan Miller think he was? He remembered being amped up. It felt good. Good to be angry at something new. Tired of the old target, the affair, how they'd almost lost each other. The cold air through the window waking him up, getting him angrier and angrier the longer they drove. He drank straight from the whiskey bottle he'd brought with him. Then . . . what happened? He searched his memory but couldn't find it.

"Claudine?"

How she looked at him said it all. The horror. The compassion. A disbelief.

Henry looked at the paper again. The article said Mr. Miller was dead. A heinous crime. A second body, a young man, Thomas James Cooke. Both dead inside the cabin.

"Henry."

She wore the silk robe he'd given her ages ago: long, pink, to the floor.

"Henry, what do you remember?"

Outside the birds were going wild, they loved the spring morning.

"Henry?"

"I remember you coming home. I remember being in the car."

"And then?"

"That's it. That's all."

"You must be repressing it," Claudine said. "That's supposed to happen with shock."

"What did I do, Claudine?"

"You were very brave."

"Tell me what I did."

"You went in yelling. Fighting. Protecting me. You pushed him. He stumbled back and fell. He got up and slugged you. Your jaw must be sore, a real one-two."

Henry touched his jaw. It felt fine, but Claudine was right. Shock. His entire body was numb.

"Then he grabbed his shotgun," Claudine said. "Before he could raise it at you, you grabbed the nearest thing you could to protect yourself, to protect me. A statue from the mantel."

This couldn't be happening to him.

"I tried to get you to stop after you hit him the first couple times. I was screaming at you to put the statue down. But you wouldn't. It was like you were in a trance. I'm sure that's why the other man came—all the screaming. He must've come back to the house between when I left the first time and when we returned. He came running out of a room in the back. He must've been asleep because he was just in his underwear. He saw the gun on the floor and went charging for it. You didn't have time to think. You grabbed it and pointed it at him and pulled the trigger. You didn't have a choice. You understand me, Henry? You didn't have a choice. He would have killed us. We would be dead right now. You saved us."

He was horrified. But he was even more horrified that he felt a punch of pride. Never had he thought he was the type of person capable of killing another human being. He had risen to the occasion. Defended her. You think you know yourself. How you'd react in a situation, but then your true nature takes over and you become someone completely different. That's the real you. Not someone—*something*. An animal. An organism. There is no reason, only reaction. In a situation like that, he would have guessed he would have run or just froze. He was a drunk. And a cuckold. That's how he saw himself. But he wasn't. He was a fighter. A survivor.

That state of being was temporary. A moment later the strange euphoria vanished. Now, in the soft light of the Aspen morning, still a little too drunk to be hungover, he was back to being himself, and that person took responsibility for their actions.

He picked up the phone.

"Who are you calling?" Claudine asked.

"The police," Henry said.

"No!" Claudine yelled, and yanked the phone from his hand.

155

"What do you mean, 'No'? We have to tell them what happened. They'll understand. Like you said, I was just defending us."

"But you went into his house, Henry. They could say you initiated it. They could say he was the one trying to defend himself. Same for the other guy."

"Yeah, but he hit you, Claudine! He beat the shit out of you! The cops will understand that the minute they see your face."

"Maybe," Claudine said. "But there's more to it."

"What do you mean?"

"You were wasted. Having a hard time walking. I put you in the car and went back in. To fix it. Your footprints and fingerprints were all over the place. The police would need a narrative. Something that made sense. Most murderers know the victims, so it would be a natural conclusion. They killed each other. Taking a stranger into your house is dangerous. A bad gamble on an employee that turned deadly."

What was she saying?

"I thought of everything. Where they would have been standing. Where they would have fallen. What would have been disrupted by the struggle before. The only conclusion will be that an argument broke out and the hired help went to kill the old man with the cowboy statue. And succeeded. But the old man got off a lucky shot before he died. Which was all it took to end his life. Both dead; no one to blame but each other."

What was she saying?

"I used my Hermès scarf—you know, the red one with the carousel horses, my prize find from the Aspen Thrift Shop—to wipe off doorknobs, countertops, anything we potentially touched. By the time I was done, there wasn't a trace of us. I burned our clothes in the fireplace as soon as we got back. This will just be our secret."

What was she saying?

"You saved me, Henry. So I saved you. Now we're both guilty. And if anyone ever finds out, we'll both have to pay for it. Don't you see? We couldn't have this be the end—not when it's so clearly the beginning."

Claudine

Recounting every detail was important. The fact that his last memory was the drive up would haunt him. She knew that. The more she could help fill in, the better.

Henry ran to the bathroom, barely making it before he got sick.

"It was the only choice we had," she said as she followed him in. She'd thought this through. Most keepers of secrets cave to someone. The urge to confess is too strong, the truth too much to handle even for the coldest heart. In order for the secret to survive, it needs tending to, needs care, or the keeper will inadvertently find ways of elevating the pressure that naturally builds, eventually giving themselves and their secret away without even realizing.

She told him this wouldn't be them. They were built differently and knew better. Think of it like an insect in a jar, Claudine explained to Henry. If there are no holes for air, inevitably the insect will thrash around, desperate to get out, to breathe. Now imagine the difference if a small hole is punched. The insect can be still; it has air. We will be each other's air.

What she didn't tell him was she was sure this could actually be good for Calhoun + Calhoun. No one wanted a property attached to such a hideous crime, and Mr. Miller didn't have any heirs. If she played it right, they could get it for pennies on the dollar at auction. They could use Kevin's and Jerry's contacts in the city to help smooth the way. It would take Henry more than a year to build the house, anyway—especially if they couldn't pour the foundation before the weather got too cold. By then the stigma associated with the lot would have sufficiently faded away.

During the immediate days after, the bond that existed between them was stronger than it had ever been. There was an urgency to their marriage. They needed each other. They now shared a secret. And their sex life was better than ever—even better than their first months of dating. Henry brought a primal dominance to the bedroom, something he'd never tapped into. It helped that he had stopped drinking—that no doubt had an impact on his sex drive—although Claudine guessed it was also a Bonnie and Clyde kind of thing: the savagery of the crime and the fact that they were able to get away with it serving as a potent aphrodisiac.

For the first few days the stories in the *Aspen Tribune* were on the front page. Claudine followed it closely with a practical eye. Henry could barely look at the paper. The sight of it brought on paralyzing moments of fear and anxiety that any second the police would knock on the door.

Details of the hired hand, Thomas James Cooke, emerged. He was originally from California. He was twenty-eight, the exact same age as Henry. According to his parents, he had spent the last few years traveling around the West, doing seasonal work and odd jobs. There was no indication when he arrived in Aspen or how long he had been working for and living with Miller. He had no prior arrest record. Young, hardworking, unlucky, dead. Bad timing was a shitty thing to die from.

Soon the stories got smaller and moved further back in the paper. By the second week they were no longer daily. There was nothing sensational about the crime to keep it newsworthy. Hardly the case of that French pop singer who killed her skier boyfriend—the one that more than a few people had mentioned to Claudine when she first moved to Aspen and they learned her name. No love affair. No financial scandal. Just two poor, lonely, solitary men living out in the middle of nowhere.

Then, nine days after the murders, the news she'd been waiting for.

PROPERTY WORKER RESPONSIBLE
FOR ASPEN LOCAL HOMICIDE

Police have determined that Jonathan Miller, 84, of Aspen, Colorado, was murdered by hired hand Thomas James Cooke, 28, permanent address unknown. Wednesday night, Mr. Miller was bludgeoned to death with a heavy object in his living room. Mr. Cooke was also killed in the struggle. It has been concluded that Mr. Miller fatally wounded Mr. Cooke with a shotgun blast in what was a last-ditch effort to retaliate from being struck. Both men were pronounced dead on the scene. Police have been unable to determine a motive, though they surmise the two men were having an argument that turned violent.

Henry

The morning after the murders, Henry made the decision, the vow, never to drink again. He took all the whiskey bottles, poured them out in the kitchen sink, and threw them in the garbage. Henry Calhoun, *killer*. This couldn't continue; he had to become someone new to outrun it. He dove into the art of self-discipline, denying himself the one thing that would help him forget it all. When every fiber of his being wanted to get tanked, desperate to reach a blackout state in which his reality was questionable, he'd go back to that morning in his mind, reading the words in the paper. Hearing Claudine's voice as she explained. He'd done something unforgivable. He focused on the pit in his stomach, knew he would have it for the rest of his life. Trying to live only in the space where it hurt most until it swallowed the urge to drink entirely. It was excruciating but sobriety was the punishment he deserved. He wanted the pain and the sickness. It was the only thing that felt right.

To not even remember the crime was unthinkable. What else had he done over the last few years when his drinking was at its worst? On more than one occasion he'd found unexplainable cuts or bruises on his hands and his legs after a hard night out. There were other things too: missing clothes, wallets, phones. He couldn't stop the most far-fetched and ridiculous thoughts. How many others were out there? How many others had he murdered and forgotten about? Maybe he was a serial killer. He would never even know.

Most days, during the first few months of sobriety, the nag came like clockwork, at happy hour. He'd sit on their balcony slowly breathing in the mountain air. The view usually calmed him. Their condo was modest but full of sunlight. Southern exposure. To fill the hours previously spent drinking, he'd been buying all kinds of plants. The green of their leaves, the pureness of the oxygen they gave off, reinforced a sense of calm. He'd focus on his new relationship with objects, with nature, how the spring trees looked like film negatives, their trunks and branches skeletally white. But soon, he knew, the leaves would come, the transformation already in the works.

Henry was also noticing how efficient and involved Claudine was in everything. While he'd been drunk, she'd worked hard; now the business was poised, ready for its first major undertaking. He'd been a terrible business partner. He could see that now. And through it all she had stood by his side. Believed in his talent. In their future. While he stewed in self-pity, unable to let her affair with Steve go, she'd doubled down.

When he thought back and tried to remember—how dark the blood must have looked as it was first coming out of Miller's head; the confused look in the young man's eye that must have been there—none of it came back to him. All he could see were flashes of driving to the house, pulling up out front, going to the door. Did he even remember going to the door? As soon as he mentally placed himself inside the cabin, all he could think about was blood. There must have been so much blood.

Then one day it was final.

"Henry. It's ours." A huge smile on her face.

"What's ours?"

"*The property.* It officially belongs to Calhoun + Calhoun."

He did not ask how. Claudine had covered up a murder. Two murders. After that, nothing she did would surprise him.

"I have a present for you," she said.

She led him into the living room and there, near the window, was a vintage oak drafting table wrapped with a bright red ribbon. He understood. It was time.

He sat down and unrolled the designs, and they never talked about any of it again.

PART FIVE

The Process of Elimination

Claudine

Breathe.
    Breathe.
    Breathe.
    It couldn't be. Could it? It was. How?

    Breathe.
        Breathe.
          Breathe.

    The wineglass slipped from her fingers, smashing into pieces. Wine spreading fast toward the rug.

Henry

The shattering of Claudine's wineglass brought Dave, the body-guard, hurrying to Zara's side.

"It's okay," she said to him, quickly grabbing Pip so she didn't walk in the glass. Then, to the rest of the group: "It's not a party until someone spills a drink!"

Zara might have been unphased by the gaff, but Claudine clearly was not. Henry saw the frozen, helpless look on her face. He knew she was mortified by the statue. It was ugly, cheap-looking. Not the sort of gift Claudine tolerated in the White Elephant. An embarrassment. Someone was intentionally trying to embarrass her, to undermine the game, to make a mockery of it in front of Zara. Henry's first guess was Steve. Maybe he wasn't responsible for the fishing package after all. Or perhaps it was whichever one of them had tipped Steve off about the party. Or maybe it was Zara, not fully comprehending the rules of the game. Whoever it was, though, Henry had to admit that Claudine's reaction was a little excessive. She just stood there. Immobile. Speechless. The bartender, towels in hand, rushed over to pick up the glass and sop up the pooling wine. Two of the waiters then rolled up the damaged rug and carried it away. Claudine hadn't moved an inch since dropping the glass, her hand slightly curled as if she still held it. After finishing the cleanup, the bartender slipped a fresh glass of wine into her hand. It took no longer than thirty seconds for everything to look as if nothing had happened. Claudine finally moved, turning to look at Henry, her eyes wide and unblinking. He couldn't remember ever seeing her so distraught. At least not since—

"What an interesting gift," Kevin said, hoping to end the awkward silence.

"Yes, what an interesting gift," Jerry said.

"Jules, who brought it?" Claudine choked out.

Jules looked at her with confusion, wondering if it was some kind of test.

"I . . . um . . . I didn't think we were supposed to say who brought the gifts," she said. "Honestly, I tried to forget who brought what as soon as I set them on the table."

"Yeah," John said, "also it's against the rules to out someone."

"I make the rules," Claudine said, "and I want to know who brought this."

No one said anything. Henry glanced at Zara, who, like everyone, seemed stunned and uncomfortable by the sternness of Claudine's voice. Claudine noticed it, too, and quickly tried to lighten her tone.

"I just think it's so unique," she said. "I'd love to know more of its provenance so people might make an informed choice about stealing it."

More awkward silence.

"I didn't bring it," said Jack Alpine. "But you can tell a little bit about it by the way the horse and rider are positioned. Can I see it for a second?"

Natalie passed the statue to her right. It made its way around the circle to Jack.

"See how the horse has one leg off the ground?" Jack said. "Means that cowboy either was hurt in a battle or died shortly after from battle injuries. Two front legs up? That rider died *in* battle."

"How do you know that?" Steve asked.

"I saw it in a civil war documentary," Jack said.

"Brother, we saw that together," Bobby said, "and I think you've got it wrong. Two front legs up and the rider died *after* battle."

"You sure?" Jack said.

"Pretty sure," Bobby said.

"Natalie, you were in the military," Jack said. "Do you know which it is?"

"They didn't teach us much in basic about the history of the cavalry," Natalie said.

"Does the U.S. Army still have a cavalry?" Rashida asked.

"So then what's it mean when the horse has all four legs on the ground?" John asked. "Does that mean the rider didn't die?"

"If anyone would like to know the history and significance of navy signal flags," Captain Tiggleman said, "I'd be happy to—"

"Enough!" Claudine shouted, once again silencing the room. The Tigglemans shifted uncomfortably. Kevin coughed. Then

Jerry coughed. Even Pip was at attention. This wasn't like her, Henry thought. She was incapable of being flustered, ruffled, rattled. She never lost her composure, even in the grimmest circumstances imaginable. Why was she getting so worked up about a stupid statue? Henry thought of how quickly the Flynns had walked away from their deal after he'd embarrassed them by passing out in the restaurant. Claudine's behavior was dangerous. How could she threaten to jeopardize their deal with Zara? What she was doing was giving Steve an opening to steal her business. Henry stood up.

"How about we take a quick five-minute break to freshen our drinks?" he said. "Can we get some music, please?"

As the pianist's hands pressed down, breaking into "Let It Snow! Let It Snow! Let It Snow!," everyone resumed their conversations, and most headed to the bar. Henry took Claudine by the arm and led her in the opposite direction, out of the living room and into the entry hall.

I was a wreck after the murders. I was twenty-two and in love for the first time in my life. The only time in my life. I hadn't experienced loss yet. Nothing had ever been taken from me before. I didn't understand what was happening, how to process it. Not only that he was gone, but that the people of this town thought he was a killer.

I told the diner I needed a little time off. I was having a hard time getting out of bed. I was lethargic. I was nauseated. I figured it was a sign of grief. Then a couple weeks after the murders I got another shock: I found out I was pregnant. I always thought a person could only be happy or sad—that one signified the absence of the other. I didn't know the two states could coexist. Certainly not with the intensity I felt them. Tommy was dead, but soon I'd have his child.

I went back and forth about going to the police. Agonized over it. The only person that knew about me and Tommy was Mr. Miller. I hadn't even told my parents. What if the real murderer found out about my connection and tried to kill me too? But knowing a baby was on the way made me determined to clear Tommy's name. I went down to the station and spoke to the detective in charge of the case. I told them they had it wrong. Tommy wouldn't hurt anyone. Mr. Miller wouldn't hurt anyone. This was all impossible.

I told him all about me and Tommy—all of the things I've said until now. The diner. Our dreams of hitting the road. The statue. The detective perked up when I mentioned the statue. He wanted me to tell him everything I knew about it and how it had ended up in the cabin. I asked him if that was what was used to kill Mr. Miller. The paper had only said he'd been bludgeoned, not with what. The detective told me he couldn't share those details, but I figured it was. I started crying. If I hadn't given Tommy the statue, maybe none of this would have happened. The detective put his hand on my shoulder and let me cry.

When I was finished, I told him I had a lead for them. There was a young woman Tommy had told me about. She had short hair and dressed very stylishly. She had been coming around the cabin trying to get Mr. Miller to sell his land. She was very persistent. Tommy kept turning her away. He told me how one time he used the rifle to shoot a box of cookies she'd brought. I told him I thought that was a bit of an overreaction, but he said she gave him a very bad feeling. The cookies incident didn't scare her off. She kept coming back.

I told the detective all this. Except about the cookies. I worried the idea of Tommy using a gun wouldn't look good. The detective dismissed me. He said, "Ma'am, do you know how many people have been trying to buy that old man out of land all these years? If we rounded 'em all up as suspects, we wouldn't have room in the jail to hold 'em all." No, they had all the evidence they needed. Clean-cut case. Domestic struggle. Go home. We're sorry for your loss.

To them, Tommy was just a hired worker. He had no status in the eyes of anyone with authority, especially the authorities. There was never a real investigation. The police didn't care. They didn't want another suspect. They weren't interested in following up on every lead. They just wanted to close the case and get the story out of the papers so that it didn't hurt tourism.

Henry

"What's wrong with you?" he asked as soon as they were alone in the hall.

"That's the statue, Henry."

"What statue?"

"The statue you killed Mr. Miller with," Claudine said.

He had no memory of it. Claudine was the one who had told him it was a statue of a cowboy. The paper had only stated Miller had been bludgeoned to death. They never said what with or printed a picture. He wondered why seeing the cowboy statue unwrapped tonight hadn't made him think of it. It was a lot smaller than the statue he had pictured. He imagined it was something big enough to have crushed the old man's head like a cantaloupe in one swift strike. The White Elephant statue wasn't that big, a little larger than his hand. No way Miller had gone down with one blow. How many times did he have to hit him? Two? Three? Which end did he use: the square base or the cowboy? Had the sharp little rifle gotten lodged in Miller's skull? Did he have to struggle to pry it out? But the main reason *this* cowboy statue hadn't immediately reminded him of *that* cowboy statue was because that was never an option. There wasn't a reality where it could be that statue. Claudine had said they would never be able to trace it to them. Locked away in an evidence room for eternity. She had promised him.

He leaned against the wall, dizzy. His breathing jagged.

"Are you sure it's the same one?" he said. "Maybe the sculptor did a series of them and this is another one."

"Don't be ridiculous," Claudine said.

"Well, maybe it's a big coincidence. What if the statue ended up in some secondhand store and somebody bought it to bring tonight, having no idea?"

"That's even more preposterous than your first idea," Claudine said. "It was a murder weapon. It was part of a police investigation. How would it end up in some secondhand store?"

"So then how?" Henry said.

"I don't know," Claudine snapped.

His fingers were numb. Hadn't the doctor said to call if his fingers went numb? Or was it his arm? No, this wasn't a coincidence. Here they were in this house. The blood house. Here they were on this land. The blood land. It knew they were there. How very dumb they'd been to think they could just walk through the door and throw a goddamn party. Why had Claudine insisted on tempting fate?

"We deserve this," Henry said.

He was cracking open.

"Look at me," ordered Claudine. She physically turned him to face her. "Stop it. Do not spiral."

Her voice sounded different now, her usual collectedness and unflappability returned.

"We need to be careful of our next move, Henry. Let's think about what's happening here. Someone brought that statue to-night. Before we ask who, let's ask why. If they know what we did, why wouldn't they go to the police?"

"They're trying to blackmail us," Henry said.

"But then why wouldn't they confront us directly? Why go through the trouble of putting the statue in the White Elephant game? That seems unnecessarily elaborate for a blackmailer. Unless that *is* the point. They want to see us squirm. They want to torture us. So, the question is: Who from this group hates us the most?"

"Us"? Henry thought. Why "us"? He wanted to say, maybe it's just you they want to destroy. Everyone hates you equally. The staff hates you because you're mean. You put them through humiliations like this stupid White Elephant game. The Alpine brothers hate you because you never appreciate their work, only tell them how it falls short. The Tigglemans hate you because they know you gouged them on the price of the last house you sold them. Kevin and Jerry hate you because you use them, constantly asking for their help with city government connections and never offer so much as a simple thank-you. Steve hates you because you used him, then dumped him. Everyone hates you as much as they possibly can, Claudine. Everyone except me. Somehow I love you. Which I guess makes me just as hateable as you. So then, yes, I suppose you are right. It is "us."

"Well, we can definitely rule out Zara," Henry said. "And also Alice, Mrs. Tiggleman, John, and Rashida. They made it pretty clear that they brought the gifts that have been opened already."

"Steve, too, then," Claudine said. "He obviously brought that fishing package."

"I don't know," Henry said. "I wouldn't rule him out. Maybe we shouldn't rule anyone out."

"But that's why you traded it with Bobby for the dice he stole from you, right?"

"Maybe that's what he *wanted* us to think. Maybe he was lying. Maybe those other four were too. People playing the game and following the poem's instructions. Like it says: 'Now is the time to put your treachery to the test.'"

They stood still, not saying anything. From the other room came the murmur of voices, stray notes from the piano. As the realization of what was happening settled in on Henry, his shock and terror were replaced by a kind of relief. It almost felt good to think there was someone else in the world who knew their secret. He had never taken one of those mail-in DNA tests but imagined it was not unlike the feeling of discovering you have an unknown relative living in another state or country. Someone was out there. Outrageous but true, there was something comforting about the thought that he and Claudine were no longer shouldering the secret on their own.

"What do we do?" he asked.

"We outplay them," Claudine said. She had shifted into battle mode.

"How?"

"We don't do anything. They want to torture us. We don't let them. We go back out there and carry on with the game. Act like everything is fine. And maybe they'll grow so frustrated with how unbothered we are that they'll say or do something to reveal themselves. The hunter will become the hunted. Let's go back. Every second we aren't there is suspicious. And it gives Steve more time to move in on Zara. From what I hear, these days he'd be lucky to get a listing in Glenwood Springs. He's not going to steal this from us."

Henry laughed to himself. He knew she had thrown in that jab at Steve for his benefit. Here she was still thinking about the sale. Her zealousness never ceased to amaze him. It knew no limits.

"There are now two goals for tonight," she said. "Sell the house to Zara and find out who brought the statue. Remember, there is no statute of limitations for murder. You could go away for the rest of your life, and they'd put me away, too, for covering it up."

Claudine touched his face.

"I didn't let it happen then and I'm not going to let it happen now. When we're a team, no one can beat us. This ends only one way. Zara with the house, us with the statue."

"That's two ways—"

"It's one *scenario*, I have the second-to-last number. I'll steal it from Natalie. I can't imagine anyone else will want that cheap thing. We can figure out how to destroy it later—along with whoever brought it. Come on."

She turned and walked toward the living room.

"Everyone back to their seats," she said, the conductor taking control of her orchestra. "Who has number eight?"

Here they were again. As if twenty years ago had never happened. The past repeating itself. Same plot of land. Same hideous secret. Same desperate attempt to conceal it. And since nothing had apparently changed, Henry figured he might as well have a drink.

Zara

I was right next to Claudine and saw every one of her face muscles clench. In the movie version of this story, the glass drops in slow motion—the shattering a metaphor of how her and Henry's lives were about to explode the same way.

Then Henry called the five-minute break and the two of them left the room. The rest of us went to the bar. By this time the snow was coming down so hard, it felt like the entire house existed inside a snow globe. Like some child had taken the world and shaken it so hard, it was impossible to tell which way was up or down. As I was staring out the windows, Steve came up to me.

"You think Aspen is beautiful now," he said, "you should see it in the spring and summer. That's the favorite time of the year for us locals. Every hillside is a blanket of wildflowers, and the rivers are fast and strong from all the melted snow. Everything is green and lush. Even the breezes are sweet. Actually, there's a listing I represent that just came on the market. A gorgeous five-bedroom that overlooks the Roaring Fork River. You should come take a look before you head back to California. I think you'd love it."

He gave me his business card, then walked away. He was a good salesman. I mean, his tan was out of control but he wasn't pushy the way Claudine was. There wasn't the same air of desperation about him. And, honestly, I was a little more receptive to his pitch than I would have been just a half hour earlier, walking out of the screening room with Henry. Once Natalie unwrapped the statue and Claudine dropped her glass, a weird energy infiltrated the house. I almost opened up my ghost hunter app to scan the room. But instead, I headed to the bar to grab a drink. The other guests had been really quiet toward me so far. I figured Claudine told them to keep their distance. Polite, but not nosey. But with her and Henry out of the room, they started to get more brave.

"Where do you write your songs?" Louisa asked.

"What's your favorite venue you've ever played?" Rashida asked.

"How do you protect your vocal cords?" Kevin asked, then Jerry asked again.

"What's the fastest quick change you've ever done during a show?" Intense John.

"Are you still in touch with Liam?" Wow. Jules was brave.

But then I was like, fuck it, and answered all of them. Told them how I've written about half my songs at Zuma Beach. The white noise of the ocean is the perfect backdrop when I'm thinking up lyrics, and that the concept of sand gives me endless inspiration. The billions of crushed shells and rock. Told them actually I loved playing at Red Rocks here in Colorado. I drink a lot of hot water with lemon and honey. I'm the master of the fifteen-second quick change. And then, unbelievably, I talked about Liam. Found myself explaining how, at the end of it, we were just different. Our takes on the world weren't compatible in the long run. I wasn't able to express myself without feeling like he was judging me. That he thought he saw the world had a right way and anyone that challenged it was foolish. It was only through saying the words that I actually figured that out for myself. I'd never be with someone who actually thought they understood what life was. Wasn't it all just this wild, unpredictable journey?

Then Claudine and Henry came back and people got quiet again. She started the game back up straightaway, and everyone drifted away from me like we hadn't been talking at all. Back to their seats.

"What can I get you?" the bartender asked me. Before I thought he was cute, but now he was really handsome. Straight teeth but crooked smile. Fucking charming. Suddenly I realized I hadn't thought that about anybody since Liam broke up with me. Another huge breakthrough. Even if I left Aspen without buying a house, the trip would be a success.

Then Henry came over to the bar. Automatically the bartender poured a club soda into a rocks glass, garnished it with lime and handed it to him. Henry had been drinking them all night. I had figured they were gin and tonics.

"No more mocktails," he said. "I'm going to need something a little harder."

"I'm sorry, sir," the bartender said. "The hostess said to only serve you nonalcoholic beverages. Her orders were strict."

"They always are," Henry said. "Tell you what. You don't have to serve me. I'll serve myself."

Henry stepped behind the bar. He put ice in the shaker, followed by vermouth and bitters. Then he gave himself a generous pour of whiskey and started shaking. Hard. I mean, in all of history ice cubes were never shaken with such force, so much purpose and determination. The bartender and I looked at each other like, *What is going on here?* It was like he was trying to start nuclear fusion.

Finally he cracked the shaker and poured its contents into a martini glass. He took a sip and let out a deep sigh, standing there with his eyes closed for a moment. Again the bartender and I exchanged a glance. Then Henry opened his eyes and said to me: "C'mon, Zara, time to meet our fate."

Being a good mother meant looking forward, not backward. Slowly I began to see my way through my anger. I'd have to let go of that. But then a couple months later I was reading the paper on a break at the diner and I saw the announcement. It was so small that I almost missed it. The newly formed boutique firm of Calhoun + Calhoun had purchased the Miller property. Though the exact sale price was not disclosed, it was rumored to be a fraction of the estimated value. Apparently there was a lack of interest due to the murders. Along with the story was a small photo of the buyers. They were a good-looking couple. She had short hair, professional and polished. He looked strong, which made more sense.

Zara

It was Jerry's turn. He didn't waste any time and ended up opening a pair of pretty sweet Prada sunglasses. He was stoked. It was funny: you could tell he didn't usually buy stuff like that—bling. He put them on and you just knew he'd sleep in them tonight. They looked good and he kept checking out his reflection in the window.

"Well, I believe I'm next," said Captain Tiggleman.

He shuffled to the table and took a brief survey, then turned to Jerry and said, "Son, I believe I'll take those sunglasses." Jerry's gasp was audible. He thought they'd never leave his face again. But there they went. What a cruel game this was.

At that moment the piano player started into "It's the Most Wonderful Time of the Year." I couldn't contain my excitement.

"Oooh, Andy Williams!" I said. "I love this song."

"Dear old Andy," Mrs. Tiggleman said. "He was a great friend. We were so sad when he passed."

"We miss him dearly," said Captain Tiggleman, "especially around this time of year."

"The most wonderful time of the year," Mrs. Tiggleman said.

"You knew Andy Williams?" I asked them.

"Oh yes," she said. "We were quite close."

"And did you know Claudine Longet too?" I asked. "I am fascinated with her."

"Of course, dear. Never has this town seen a more beautiful woman. Until your arrival tonight."

"Shame we don't see her anymore," Mr. Tiggleman said. "But after the murder she became very withdrawn. Estranged even from her oldest friends."

"What murder?" Jules asked.

"You've never heard of the Spider Sabich murder?" Bobby Alpine said.

A few of the other young Calhoun + Calhoun agents said they hadn't either. I quickly, excitedly ran it down for them. The White Elephant was temporarily halted. Everyone sat listening, riveted. Even Dave came in from the kitchen to hear.

"Claudine Longet was from another planet," said Captain Tiggleman after I'd finished my recap. "Simply being in her presence was both the most exciting thing that had ever happened to you and the most devastating, since you were likely never to have the chance to know her. I mean truly know her. I'm not even sure if Andy ever knew her. Or if she knew herself. She was like a promise of a promise that would never come true."

"Do you think she meant to kill Spider?" I asked.

Mrs. Tiggleman tried to raise her eyebrows as much as her plastic surgery would allow, then sighed.

"I'm not sure. When you get to my age, if you're lucky, you realize you can't ever understand why people do what they do. Did she kill him? Yes. Had they been on the verge of a breakup? Maybe. Was she out of her mind that Sunday afternoon? Perhaps."

"The diaries, right?" I asked. "The ones that were inadmissible in court. Supposedly they indicated her deep, deep unhappiness—"

"It would take more than a few diary entries expressing unhappiness to convince me she killed him with great intent," Mrs. Tiggleman said, sounding like someone who had made a few diary entries of her own expressing unhappiness. "No, I don't believe she did."

"And Andy certainly didn't," said Mr. Tiggleman. "Which was good enough for us."

"This town is full of crazy stories like that," said Kevin. "There was Ted Bundy killing Caryn Campbell, then escaping from the Pitkin County Courthouse."

"Then, after they caught him and transferred him to Glenwood Springs, he escaped again," said Jack Alpine.

"Full of crazy stories like that," Jerry said. "The murder of Nancy Pfister."

"Yeah, that was awful," Louisa said. "I mean, they found her in a suitcase."

"It was a trash bag," Rashida corrected.

"And of course the two murders that happened right on this very property," Bobby Alpine said.

"Who could forget that one?" Steve chimed in.

"That's right," Mrs. Tiggleman said. "Jonathan Miller and that young boy. Don't remember his name. I nearly forgot about that."

"Who is Jonathan Miller?" I asked.

"It's a horrible story," Mr. Tiggleman.

"Very gruesome," Jack Alpine.

I wasn't looking at Claudine or Henry just then but I wish I had been. I wish I would've seen what their reaction was.

Claudine

Claudine sat in horror listening to various members of the group recount the Miller murders. None of them could remember the details exactly.

"A double suicide, wasn't it?"

"No, the kid tried to kill the old man for money and the old man fought back."

"I thought it was the other way around. I thought Miller was the aggressor and the kid was defending himself."

"I just remember hearing the cabin was drenched in blood, like when the elevator doors open in *The Shining*."

Whoever had brought the statue to the White Elephant— was this part of their plan? Was this another phase of their torture? Bobby Alpine had been the one to first mention it. But would he reveal himself so blatantly?

"The only one who made it out of that travesty alive was Claudine and Henry," Steve said.

Claudine looked at Henry. He had a glass of something brown in his hand. How easy, how weak of him. That stupid bartender. She told him not to let Henry drink. She watched him tilt the glass all the way back, swallow the liquid in one gulp, and head back for a refill. Well, forget counting on him.

She worried her silence was incriminating. She remembered what she had told Henry: Outplay the player.

"Better than alive," she said. "You wouldn't believe how cheap we were able to get this land. Everyone was scared off by the murders. Developers never thought anyone would want to live on a property with such a sordid history. But this is the American West. Show me a piece of land that hasn't had blood spilled on it. Do you know how many bodies are buried in these mountains? Between the Utes and the miners, this entire state is a graveyard."

"A graveyard with a very expensive lift ticket." Good, if she let Steve talk long enough he was bound to embarrass himself like this poor, tasteless joke that fell flat.

"It's true," Kevin said as he selected a gift from the table. "So many merciless stories."

"Very true," Jerry said.

"Henry and I knew that people have short memories. Eventually they'd be willing to overlook what happened here for the sake of the view. And we were right. When we sold the house to the Lions, we made back twenty times our original investment. What's the most you ever profited from a sale, Steve?"

She took a sip from her glass. Kevin and Jerry were jumping up and down, Kevin having unwrapped front-row seats and backstage passes to Zara's MGM show next fall. The celebration didn't last long, because Steve's turn was next and he took them.

"Give those back to Kevin." Henry's voice was loud. But it

was too late to stop him. "I'm sorry—or actually I'm *not* sorry. Steve, you were not invited here. Look around this room, every person, every *guest*, received something called an invitation. Do you know what that means? You think everything is *yours*. Everything is *not* yours. Do you hear me? Can you understand that?"

"You're drunk, Henry," Steve said dismissively. Then he turned to Zara. "It really only matters what you think. Would you be comfortable living in the same spot where two people savagely killed each other?"

The whole room turned to look at Zara.

"Well, as long as the place isn't haunted, right?"

And just as she said that, the lights went out.

Months later, I went back to see the detective—the one I had spoken to before. I knew it was pointless to mention the sale of the land to the Calhouns. That wasn't why I was there.

I told him about my situation. Not that I needed to. I was eight months pregnant and huge. I sensed that he felt sorry for me. He believed Tommy was a killer and that one day I would have to explain this to my child. I used his sympathy to my advantage. I asked him about the statue. What happened to that kind of evidence when a case was closed? Was there any way I could get it back? My father had sculpted it and I wanted to pass it down to his grandchild.

He said usually they kept that kind of evidence permanently. I just stood there looking at him until he sighed and left the room. When he came back, he had the statue in a clear Ziploc bag. I didn't even have to sign a piece of paper.

I wasn't lying. This was an heirloom, I wanted my child to feel a connection to our ancestry. But I also wanted it in case the time ever came that it could be used it to clear Tommy's name. I had no idea how that could happen. Certainly not without putting myself in jeopardy. The Calhouns were dangerous people. They couldn't be underestimated. But maybe one day an opportunity would present itself. Maybe one day the statue could be used to bring them down. To find some justice.

Henry

They were all in on it.

That was what Henry was thinking as the group discussed the Miller murders.

Wasn't that how that Agatha Christie train mystery ends? They all did it? So fed up with Claudine's bullshit, they had banded together and came up with this scheme to ruin the two of them in the most cruel way possible? Maybe they hired Zara to play her part. He'd heard of pop stars getting paid seven figures to play birthday parties for rich people. Maybe Zara cut them a deal, since it was for a good cause: finally bringing the Calhouns to justice.

Henry took a big swig of his Manhattan. He forgot how much he missed making a good cocktail. He loved all the steps, how methodical you had to be. The ice, the pour, the clink of the shaker top, the adultery. The shake, the ice, the pour, the homicide. The clink of the spoon, the twist of orange, the double homicide. The splash of the cherry on a toothpick when it hit the drink, signaling it was ready. The bartender didn't have any toothpicks. One detail Claudine managed to overlook. The party was toothpick-less. But the drink still tasted wonderful. Closing his eyes, he took another long, necessary sip. The warmth spread throughout his body, a reunion he thought would never come. An old friend.

He got up to get another one. Then the lights went out, plunging the room into semi-darkness. The flames of the fire and scattering of candles the only sources of light. Gasps and nervous whispers. Pip started barking. Dave quickly hurried to Zara's side. In the limited light, the outside became much brighter, the trees and mountains gaining an eerie definition visible through the snow.

"Must be the storm," Jack Alpine said. "Knocked out power."

"Do we have any more candles?" Mrs. Tiggleman said.

"I'll get them," Henry said. "I'm already up."

"I know where they are," Jules said. "I'll go with you."

The two of them walked down the hall toward the kitchen.

"They're in here," Jules said, opening a side door. "In the pantry."

She quickly shoved him inside, and unsuccessfully flipped the light switch a few times. Nothing. Still, she closed the door. The space was cramped, just barely enough room for the two of them. It smelled of spices and her perfume. Henry felt along the top shelf and found the box of dinner candles. He struck a long match on the side of the box and lit one.

"Henry," Jules said, "I need to confess something. I . . . I know what happened."

She knows what happened? She was the last person Henry would have guessed. Which of course made her the obvious choice. Wasn't that also how it worked in those Agatha Christie books? The kindest, gentlest character turned out to be the duplicitous mastermind. It was ironic: all those late nights in the office, he'd been tempted to tell her, and he didn't have to. She already knew. Now he was what, supposed to confess? Redeem himself a tiny bit by turning himself in?

"How did you find out?" he asked.

"Everybody in the office talks about it behind your back," she said.

"What? Everybody knows? Why hasn't anyone said anything?"

"They don't want to embarrass you. It happened so long ago. They figure it isn't their business."

Henry was confused.

"Jules, what are you talking about?"

"Claudine's affair with Steve. Wait a second, you did know, right? Oh god, please tell me you knew."

The entire office knew about Claudine and Steve. That wasn't what he was expecting to hear. It was the first time anyone had ever acknowledged Claudine's affair out loud. He was surprised how painful it was to hear it, even after so many years.

"Yes," he said. "I knew."

"She just disgusts me so much. How could she treat you like that? That's why I invited Steve tonight. I wanted to make this night insufferable for her. I want her to lose the sale to Zara. And I guess I figured if I put all of you in the same room, it'd help you see that you deserve better."

"Invited Steve? So you didn't bring the statue?"

"The statue? No. I brought a star. Literally a star. You get to name an actual star. Why? What does the statue have to do with anything?"

He put his hand to his head. It felt like the pantry was shrinking, the walls closing in on them.

"I need another drink," Henry said.

"No," she said, "what you need is to make a fundamental change in your life. What you need is to leave Claudine."

He knew she was right. He knew that quitting tomorrow and leaving the state or even the country wouldn't be enough. Not if Claudine was with him. If he had any chance of making a fresh start, it would need to be without her. But he knew he never would. "Till death do us part." That was the vow he had made. Only death hadn't parted them. What would he be without her, she'd been part of his sense of self for so long.

"I'm young," Jules said. "I know. But I think the world is this weird, wonderful place, and you never know when something—someone—extraordinary will come along and change your life."

Henry put his hands on her shoulders. Jules closed her eyes and tipped her head back, expecting a kiss. The image flashed in his mind of wrapping his hands around her throat and squeezing tight. Eyes bulging. Gasping for air. Struggling to pull his fingers away. That was the sort of thing he was capable of. That was what lived deep inside of him. He kissed her on the forehead and took a step back. She knew what that meant.

"Okay," she said, taking the box of candles from the shelf. "My guess is Claudine brought that statue. Everyone knows the company's in bad shape. She probably couldn't afford a fancy gift. So she got a crappy one to blame on someone else. You saw how over-the-top her reaction was. What an actress. Then you watch: she'll steal it, say she's sacrificing herself for the group, and come out looking like a hero. Better get back with these." Then she was gone.

Henry stood there in the pantry, frozen. It made so much sense. There wasn't a photo or a mention of the murder weapon in the paper because maybe the murder weapon was never found. Claudine had hung on to it all these years, just in case she needed to keep Henry in check, remind him she was in control of his fate. Now he was talking about quitting the company? Putting the statue in the White Elephant was her way of reminding him that she was the one who made those decisions. They were finished only when she said they were finished.

He was embarrassed he hadn't figured it out sooner. Now that he had, though, he had the upper hand. But upper hand to do what? "We have to outplay them," Claudine had said. He had no idea how to do that or what that even meant. He went to get another drink and think it over before heading back to the game. How was he supposed to outplay her?

Claudine

Of course it had crossed Claudine's mind that Henry might've brought the statue. He was the *first* person she thought of. All that talk about quitting the business and leaving the state. If he had somehow managed to get his hands on it, wouldn't that put him in a pretty little spot to ask of her anything he wanted? Dangling the old murder weapon in front of her. Reminding her he could throw away everything in a minute. Threatening to tell the world what they had done so she'd set him free. She hadn't listened to him when he tried to talk to her about it. Maybe this was the only way he could get her attention and force her to take him seriously.

But she had immediately ruled him out based on his initial reaction. First his cluelessness, then his fear: it seemed genuine. Then his drinking. If he was in control he wouldn't slip up like that. But he had proven to be a surprisingly good liar. Honestly, she never thought he'd be able to keep their secret all these years. She thought for sure he'd crack, wind up in the hospital with a nervous breakdown a lot sooner than he did.

When he scampered off with Jules to get the candles was when she finally took him seriously as a suspect. No, she never believed he would cheat on her. But then, she never believed she'd ever see that statue again. Tonight had proven that anything was possible. Was Jules in on it with him? Had she coached him on how to react? When he said he wanted to leave town, was it Jules he was planning on taking rather than Claudine?

As everyone sat around in uncomfortable silence waiting for them to get back with the candles, Claudine felt a longing for her husband that she had never felt before, not even that night in the forest when she first set eyes on Miller's cabin. Then came a voice:

> *It's a lonely time to live through*
> *How do you expect anyone to have any fun*

Zara was singing.

Zara

When the lights went out I got super freaked out. I mean, I had just asked if Montague House was haunted. And then, *bam*, I'm surrounded by pitch-black in a snow storm? No way. Nu-uh. I would've grabbed Dave and we would have gotten the hell out of there, but I hadn't picked my gift yet. I was 100 percent not buying this house that was possessed by two ghosts who'd killed each other, but I figured I'd come all the way to Aspen, so I shouldn't go home empty-handed. I deserved something for my trouble.

When I'm afraid, I grab Pip. And when I'm still afraid, I sing. So that's what I did. I picked an old Claudine Longet holiday song called "I Don't Intend to Spend Christmas Without You." It was originally written and performed by this American folksinger Margo Guryan, but Claudine's rendition is much more mournful. The piano player knew it, because after the first few lines he started playing along.

When it ended, everybody stood up and started clapping. Then Jules and Henry came in carrying lit candles—and a fresh cocktail for Henry. I'm not one to count drinks, but he seemed to be hitting it pretty hard.

Finally the game continued. At this point we were about halfway through. I don't remember all the specifics of who picked what, especially in light of what happened next. The time immediately before is kind of foggy. Basically, my tickets and backstage passes got stolen as much as possible. Henry didn't have to worry about Steve getting them. Eventually they wound up with Rashida. Then it was Claudine's turn. She picked right before me.

"Well," she said, "I know how important tonight is to every-one, and I'm not about to let one of you go home with a joke. So, Natalie, I'll take the statue, please."

I saw Jules look at Henry and raise her eyebrows like, *See?* Henry tipped his glass to her and drank all of it.

Natalie looked relieved and went and picked from the table. Then it was my turn. I couldn't help making it a bit dramatic. That's part of my job, after all.

"Henry, Claudine, thank you for having me. It has been a true pleasure to spend the evening with all of you, to experi-ence Montague House so full of life. And poltergeists. As the last pick of the night, there could only be one gift for me. In the true spirit of the game, I'm going to steal . . . from Claudine."

I walked over and took the statue from her. Everyone went crazy.

"Ooooooh."

"Daaaamn."

"No way."

Even Dave said, "That's cold."

Claudine looked startled, then glared at everyone. They immediately went quiet.

"Zara, why on earth would you want that statue?"

"Why *wouldn't* I want it? Look at it. It's so kitschy. I love stuff like this."

And I did. But there was another reason. I kept looking at it. It had a mesmerizing quality, this strange gravitational pull on me. I wasn't sure where the statue came from but it just looked like it had an interesting story. And also I loved the fact that, unlike the rest of the gifts, it hadn't been brought to please Claudine. In fact, it was the opposite. Someone really wanted to piss her off. I appreciated how anarchic and rock-and-roll that was.

"Zara, please," Claudine said. "Look around. There's a room full of treasures."

There was a weird desperation in her voice. She was sounding a little manic. "Go on, everyone, hold them up. Show Zara what her options are." Everyone awkwardly held up their gifts. "How about the Portuguese tapestry? I was thinking it would look nice hanging upstairs in the master bathroom. The wall across from the claw-foot tub is made for it. The room is beautiful, but it could stand for a splash of art. Imagine it, the southern light bringing out the blues and the blue-greens? Louisa, please take Zara the tapestry."

"No, Louisa," I said. "Stay where you are. Claudine, I'm sorry, but I'm not going to be buying this house. It's gorgeous." I turned to Henry. "A true work of art. But there's no connection. I know when I know. The statue and I have a connection. And I'd like to take it home with me."

"No," she said. "I'm sorry, but no. That's just not possible. You can either choose another gift or take the last one on the table."

"But there are two gifts on the table," Captain Tiggleman said.

This has been a lot. I know. But I had to make sure you understood that you come from an unusual, brief love that ended in tragedy before it ever even had a chance to understand what it fully was. Never doubt it was love. Never doubt that whatever really happened on the mountain that night, Tommy would never hurt Mr. Miller. Every single part of me, every instinct, knows that the Calhouns had something—maybe everything—to do with it all.

I made my choice not to let the injustice consume me. Somehow I found the strength to not only continue but to live a life. I hope you find your own strength in that.

Grow up knowledgeable, but choose the path that is uniquely yours. Uncertainty is normal. Keep going. Eventually, it will start to take shape. It will feel right. You will know. And every time you need me, remember: I'm always here. In the air and the river, in all of nature. But mainly in you. We are the same. All three of us. Don't worry, I'm here. Cheering you on. Your father is here too.

Love,
Mom

Claudine

Claudine thought it might just be Captain Tiggleman's poor vision in the dim candlelight, but he was right. There was an extra gift on the table.

"Jules!" she seethed.

"No way," Jules said. "That's not possible. We had fifteen. Then Steve made it sixteen. I counted like five times."

"Miscount!" Jerry yelled. "I guess we have to start again. I'll have to part with my Bootsy Bellows gift certificate."

"We'll have to start again," Kevin said.

Claudine felt twitchy. She, too, had counted the gifts. She didn't trust Jules to be the final say on anything. To get the count correct. There had been sixteen. Then she read the poem and they started. Everyone was there. No one else had arrived.

Confused whispers swirled around the room. Laughter, shouts of "Let's draw straws to see who gets the last gift!" Everyone was drunk. What was she missing? It was as she made her third scan around the room that it hit her.

Why hadn't she seriously considered this earlier?

Yes. Of course.

She found him instantly and they locked eyes across the room. The rest of them oblivious, the unofficial post-gift swap already starting. The look on his face was all the confirmation she needed. He had his jacket on. His hood was up. He had been waiting for her to understand, it had only been a matter of time.

Paces behind, she followed him out of the living room, down the hall, and into the kitchen. Getting her own jacket from the closet along the way. She entered the kitchen just as the handsome young man slid open the door to the deck and slipped through, leaving it ajar.

The chef had his back turned, plating the last of the desserts, and she took a small, sharp paring knife off a cutting board. The contours of the hilt fit perfectly in the palm of her hand, like the hand of an old dance partner. She slipped the serrated blade snuggly up the long sleeve of her Alexander McQueen blouse. Pressed against her flesh, the cold metal stung lightly, raising the tiny hairs on her arm. It had been years since she'd felt this sort of charge.

Then she was gone into the night after the bartender.

Henry

Jules was right. It had to be Claudine who brought the statue.
But she was wrong about why. The motive wasn't shielding her
guests from a bad present. It was to send him a message. Keep
him in line. She had concocted an impressive, elaborate scheme
to intimidate him. She had thought of everything. Except Zara
wanting the statue. That's when she slipped up. Trying so hard
to keep it from Zara. She never imagined that. Now their murder weapon was in the hands of a stranger. And not just any
stranger. One of the most famous people on the planet. Henry
could just see the tabloid photos of Zara returning home to
L.A. with the statue under her arm and how wild social media
would go with rumors about what it was. Look at how those
true-crime junkies and amateur detectives online managed to
solve the Golden State Killer case. It wouldn't take long for people to figure it out. Him and Claudine put away by a pop star's
super-groupies. He had to admit, it was pretty funny.

At least, it would be if that was how it happened. There
wasn't a chance Zara would be leaving with the statue. Clau-

dine wasn't one to accept her fate, most likely she already had a plan. Not until she had it. Henry was worried about Zara, but he was also worried about Claudine. He couldn't help it. The bodyguard would need distracting, the dog, the guests—if she was going to pull something off there were a lot of details to contend with. She would need his help.

Henry looked around for her. They needed to talk. To figure this out. Together. Like she said, nobody could beat them when they worked as a team.

He caught a glimpse of her as she followed someone out of the living room. He couldn't tell who it was. Someone in a coat with an upturned hood. A new recruit? Drink in hand, he started for the door.

Claudine

She edged along the deck wall, keeping under the overhang where the footing was more sure. Although even there it was slippery. It was snowing from every direction. The Adirondack chairs, the firepits, the grill—all of it was covered in a thick blanket of white. Near the far edge of the deck, down on the lower level, the hot tub was bubbling uncovered, eating as much snow as it could. She tried to figure out where he was, but the wind gusts kept blowing snow in her face every time she turned to look in a new direction.

She spotted him. Near the far edge he was leaning back against the railing, waiting for her. The wind howled and whined as she made her way over. He didn't say anything, only stared with hatred.

"How much do you want?" Claudine asked.

"How much what?"

"Money."

The bartender laughed.

"That's the only thing you people think about, isn't it?" he said. "I don't want your money."

"What do you want?"

"Confirmation. The truth, and I'd say I got it."

Claudine moved her hand slightly so she could feel the tip of the dagger pressed against the soft inside skin of her arm. The pinch from the blade sending another shock through her body.

"Coming into tonight, I still had some doubt," he said. "She told me your names. In the letter. It had to be you. I questioned if tonight would work. Doubted I could stand there in front of you both and pretend like I was just some regular bartender. Follow your directions for twenty dollars an hour. Pour your drinks and smile. I didn't know how long I'd last. Thought you'd find something suspicious even before the gift was opened. There were too many variables."

"What in the hell are you talking about?" Claudine shouted at him through the snow.

"It could have unfolded so many ways. If it was picked much later in the game. Or not at all. There was even a chance it could have been the extra gift on the table. Maybe it wouldn't have been opened. This has been in the works. I heard about your office party game; hell, the whole town has. But it took me a couple years to figure out properly how to pull this off."

He boldly took a step toward her.

"You should have seen your face when that girl opened it. There were times when I thought about confronting you straight up. Coming to your office or stopping you on the street. But it definitely wouldn't have been as sweet as that look. As your face. No, this was the only way. What was it like? Have you ever felt a paranoia that deep? That's what my mother felt every day of her short life after what you did. Knowing that you walked the same streets."

"Your mother? Who was your mother?"

"That's not the right question," the bartender said.

"Your father?" Then she smiled, having put it together. "Your father was the hired hand."

"Thomas James Cooke," he said.

"Oh, that's interesting," Claudine said. "Very interesting. You must be clever. Or *someone* was clever. I have to know: How did you get the statue?"

The bartender told her.

"Aspen cops," she said. "Too nice for their own good. That's how Bundy escaped. They didn't cuff him and he jumped right out the window of the Pitkin County Courthouse."

"You can see if it's still open. You'll be there soon enough."

A gust of wind tore between them, both having to momentarily turn and shield their faces.

"That's how you think this ends?" she said. "Sorry to disappoint. The police had the statue back then and it didn't make any difference. So unless you've got a confession—"

The bartender took his hand out of his jacket pocket. He was holding a small digital voice recorder. Hardly surprising. She counted on it. And yet she hadn't spoken carefully or avoided saying anything that could be held against her in court. What did she care? She would get that device from him just as surely as she would get that statue from Zara.

Claudine took a step toward him, inching the knife out of

her sleeve. "Why so much drama?" she asked. "You should have swung by the office. We could have talked."

"I'm not dumb. What could be better than this? A house full of your friends and employees plus a super famous pop star and her enormous bodyguard. The stakes are too high for you to pull anything here. But alone? Not a chance. Who's to say your husband wouldn't try and kill me like he did my father and Mr. Miller?"

"My husband?"

Claudine began laughing. Laughing and laughing. The bartender looked uncertain.

"What's so funny?" he asked.

"You think my husband is a killer?"

"I *know* he is," the bartender said. "And, given the chance, I'm sure he'd kill again."

Claudine unsheathed the knife from her sleeve. He was backed into a corner, the only options to jump off the deck and over a cliff or go straight through her.

"Henry kill again?" she said. "That would mean he's killed before. Henry didn't kill your father. I did."

Henry

He'd been wrong. It was only the bartender she followed outside. No doubt to yell at him about Henry's drinking. He was about to call out to her, tell her to lay off, leave the kid alone, this was his fault, when their voices reached him. He stood and listened.

"Henry kill again? That would mean he's killed before. Henry didn't kill your father. I did."

What was she saying? And why was she saying it to the bartender? He didn't understand. The booze wasn't helping. But still, he wrapped his fingers tighter around his drink, processing what he'd overheard.

"Claudine?"

Her back flinched when she heard her name.

"Claudine. What's going on?"

She turned around. The knife blade flashed in her hand.

"Henry, dear, meet—I'm sorry, I didn't get your name."

"Thomas," the bartender said. He looked frightened.

"Well, of course it is," Claudine said. "Henry, this is Thomas

James Cooke. He's named after his father. Who you killed. No, I'm sorry, *whom* I killed?"

"Who you killed?" A queasiness spread through him.

"Henry, do you really think that you—*you*—beat an old man to death? Pounded in his head, then grabbed a shotgun and unloaded it into the strong young man who was coming to his aid? That's truly comical. You did what you always did. What's in your very nature. Even tonight. You drank. You were drunk when I found you at the house and you drank yourself to sleep in the car. Passed out by the time we arrived. Exactly what was supposed to happen. You played your role perfectly."

There it was. An answer to something that had always bothered him. This was why she hadn't complained about his drinking before the murders. But it didn't answer everything.

"I don't understand why—"

"Stop saying that," she cut him off. "You *do* understand. You can't always run around not understanding. Try harder, Henry. Try harder to understand. If I hadn't done it, our entire lives never would have happened."

"Why did you have to kill them?"

"I was tired of waiting, Henry! What can I say? I'm impatient. Same reason I fucked Steve. And this whole exchange is growing tedious."

A horrible thought came over Henry.

"That night when you came home . . . did Mr. Miller even hit you?"

"Sure he did. The same way young Thomas here beat me up tonight."

"I haven't touched you," Thomas said.

"Hmmm, let's see. I haven't had much time to think. The

Miller story took me a couple weeks to come up with. But here it goes: The game finished and I was coming out for air. You were, what?" Claudine glanced toward a tub full of champagne bottles keeping cold outside. "You were grabbing more champagne. Then what? You tried to force yourself on me. No, too cliché. Too generic. A good lie is about the details. You wanted more money. Were unhappy with the tip I gave you. Obsessed with the night's casual display of wealth. Jealous of all the incredible gifts that were opened. That's better. You lashed out and threw me against the pillar."

At that, Claudine violently smashed her forehead onto a corner of the nearby support beam. It cut through her skin instantly. Dark, pitch-black blood gushed down her face.

"Jesus!" cried Thomas.

Henry was too stunned to speak.

Claudine

"I was scared for my life," Claudine continued. "I've never been so afraid. But Thomas had set this knife down by the champagne."

She used her knife as a pointer as she spoke.

"Earlier it was helpful cutting off the foil caps on the champagne before bringing them inside. That was it. I walked out and made a comment about the knife. Joked how sharp those things were. He told me the blade on his wine opener was too dull. See what I mean? Details. After he hit me, it was pure luck that I got to the knife first. It could have gone either way. I just stabbed what I could and happened to catch an artery. A simple case of self-defense."

Panic flashed in Thomas's eyes. Claudine's face was a bloody wreck. She made it worse by repeatedly smearing it so it wouldn't blur her vision. Henry was having trouble breathing. He was clutching his arm.

"No, Claudine," he said.

"You're right, Henry," she said. "You're so right. It's much more believable if you do it. Just like it was for the Miller story. Much more likely that you'd overpower this strong young man. Get to the knife first. Come to think of it, Thomas, you're about the same age as your father was then. That kind of symmetry might get you an extra write-up in the *Aspen Tribune*. How about this: Henry, noticing I've been gone from the party too long, comes out to find me. He sees the bartender toss me into the pillar, grabs the knife, and without thinking plunges it into his chest. A hero."

The bartender made a motion to get past Claudine, but she instantly countered, blocking his way.

"Henry, here is your chance. You always thought you were a murderer. Tonight you finally get to become one."

Laying the knife flat on her palm, she offered the blade to Henry.

"You know exactly what you have to do."

Henry

He looked at the knife, then at Thomas, then back at the knife.

The sound of familiar carols crept out from inside.

"Deck the halls with boughs of holly / Fa-la-la-la-la, la-la-la-la . . ."

His left arm was completely numb now. His heart slamming in his chest.

"Henry, this will end it once and for all," Claudine said. "You want to retire? Close up shop? You want to leave Aspen? Let's do it. But we can't leave any loose ends. You have to do this."

He tried to slow his breathing but couldn't. He was gulping for air now.

"No, Claudine," Henry said between gasps. "There isn't a world that exists where I kill him."

"Fine," Claudine said. "Then I will."

With a quick flip of her wrist she now held the knife the proper way. Blade out, she lunged at the bartender.

"No!" he yelled, rushing at her. He grabbed her knife hand, and fought to wrench the weapon away.

"Let go of me!" she said, thrashing to break free.

He managed to hold his arms up, protecting himself and pushing her to the side, throwing her off-balance so that she landed in the snow.

There would be no atonement, he knew that. Keeping her from killing Thomas would never change the fact they had killed his father. And yes, it was both of them who had done it. Claudine might have been the one who swung the statue and fired the rifle, but Henry stayed silent. Weak. He was to blame. If he could get the knife out of her hand, he and Thomas could take her. Two on one. Hold her down until the police arrived. He was ready to accept the consequences. Ready to tell them everything. The nightmare would be over.

Suddenly he staggered backward, clutching his chest. He tried to steady himself by holding on to one of the deck chairs but lost his grip and collapsed like a felled tree into the soft white powder, his heart stopping before he hit the ground.

Claudine

There was a brief moment of silence as Claudine waited for him to rise, but the outline of his body was very still. He didn't get up. Without taking her eyes from Thomas, or lowering the knife, she knelt by Henry's side. His face was still warm. Stealing a glance, she saw his eyes half open, staring blankly. No pulse. Her pain was sharp. Just like that, their chapter ends. They were over. Since the day they met, she'd actually never imagined her life without him.

"Poor Henry," she said. It was the sudden peal of laughter from inside that jarred her back. "I wouldn't have enjoyed killing him. This way he goes out as more of a hero than a victim. People will remember his bravery. His funeral will be well attended. Not yours, though."

She raised the knife high above her head.

"No," Thomas pleaded. "You don't have to do this. Please."

A million thoughts flooded through her. She'd whip up some tears and run back into the party. She'd struggle to get the words out. *Bartender . . . slammed me . . . Henry . . . tried to stop him . . . heart attack . . . grabbed the knife . . . stabbed him . . .* The investigation would be quick. Unlike the Miller murders, they had witnesses. The party guests. They would believe her. It might take a little while for the house to sell, to escape another blemish of tragedy, but eventually it would. People always forgot. Even though Zara was a lost cause, Claudine would still get notoriety. She'd be known as a fighter, a survivor. Maybe she'd appear on talk shows, get a book deal, go on the lecture circuit. She'd be bigger than ever. She'd have to change the stationery and the sign on the office door. What would she call it? Not Calhoun Realty. Something more ambitious. The Calhoun Agency. That was better. Or maybe the Calhoun Company. The alliteration was a nice touch—

Hit from behind, Claudine dropped to the ground.

Zara stood over her body, breathless. She was holding the cowboy statue she'd hit her with. Already there was a light dusting of snow on Henry who lay by her side. They'd fallen in a V shape, their hands reaching for each other's but not touching. Pip scurried over and sniffed them. Pomeranians aren't known to spontaneously howl, but the dog tipped her tiny face up to the sky and let out a sorrowful song.

Zara

Listen, I don't consider myself a hero, but I know a lot of people do.

I'd been looking for the bartender, to say goodbye. Fine, to slip him my number. That's the only reason I went out there. From the living room, none of us could see Claudine and Henry and Thomas arguing. The snow was coming down too hard. And you couldn't hear them, either, thanks to the soundproof triple-paned picture windows Henry had originally installed in the house. Plus there was so much commotion about the extra present and everyone deciding what to do next. People were pretty tipsy. They all started caroling, even gathering around the piano and singing "Deck the Halls."

I can't tell you what I was thinking when I hit Claudine. I wasn't thinking anything. I just reacted. The statue was small but heavy. Like, twice what one of my Grammys weighs. I caught her right at the base of the neck, which was probably good. Any higher up and I might've killed her like she did with the old man. I'm not sure how I would've handled killing some-one, even someone as nasty as Claudine. Not just the murders but lying about Mr. Miller's abuse and planning to do the same with Thomas. That's so disgusting. If I had killed Claudine, she never would have been dead. Killing her would have linked her to me forever.

At first I felt responsible for Henry's death. If we'd been able to get the paramedics there sooner, maybe they could have saved him. I wasn't getting cell service because of the storm, neither was Thomas, and apparently Claudine had locked away everyone else's phones in the house safe. Nobody knew the combination. I had Dave pry it open with the fireplace stoker. Once they were called, it took them a while to get there, the roads were terrible. That night turned out to be a historic snowfall for Aspen. It missed breaking the single-day record by like an inch. When the paramedics finally arrived, they confirmed that Henry was dead; later on an autopsy indicated his heart had stopped cold. It was quick and probably painless.

Claudine was just starting to come out of it. We had moved both her and Henry into the living room. There was a big conversation about whether or not that was the right thing to do. We had all seen enough crime shows to know you're not supposed to touch any evidence at an actual crime scene. But Thomas and I had witnessed the whole thing. There was no mystery to solve. What were we going to do, leave them in the snow? We didn't want Claudine to freeze to death, and it didn't feel right with Henry out there by himself with the snow piling on top of him. Thomas took a video of the scene before we moved them, in case the police needed it for reference.

We also had a conversation about whether or not Claudine should be tied up. That one was much shorter. We agreed it was a smart move. It felt like there was a real chance she would wake up and somehow manage to take us all out. So Captain Tiggleman used some salvaged ribbon to tie her hands and feet in what he called a bowline knot. I'm pretty sure it was the ribbon from Henry's gift. Somewhere in the mix Rashida had opened a set of three rare broken tulip bulbs. They weren't broken-broken, that's just the name of them. Jules told us they were his favorite. The broken kind bloomed in multicolored patterns, their beauty the result of a virus. During their brief life they are beautiful but sick and die early. For a while I couldn't figure out which Claudine's was, but after Steve stole my tickets from Kevin, he'd ended up with her gift. It was fitting. Six runs heli-skiing in the Elk Mountains. People were saying it wasn't even legal, but somehow she'd arranged it. There's no way Kevin's doing a chopper drop. My guess is it went to waste.

The police showed up at the same time as the paramedics. They took statements from all of us. It was surreal. Then, soon everyone started to leave. I stuck around. I still wanted to give Thomas my number, and the police kept him the longest. I was there when he showed them the letter from his mom and explained about the statue. Once again the cops bagged it as evidence. I asked them if I could have it back when they were done with it. They said they'd let me know. It's been six months and I haven't heard anything. Looks like they're being extra cautious after hearing how easily Thomas's mom got it back.

I'd be lying if I said the past six months haven't been intense. Only now has the news coverage started dying down. I thought I had it bad with the paparazzi before. I had no idea. They were after me twenty-four seven. We even had to bring on a couple extra security guys to help Dave out. Being in the center of a story like this has totally made me rethink my obsession with Claudine Longet and true crime in general. It seems so interesting and almost sexy when you're looking in from the outside, watching it on a screen. You're a voyeur. It's entertainment. But when you're on the *inside*, when you're directly involved with a case of humanity gone bad? There's nothing sexy about it. It's not fun to follow and shout out ideas and theories. It's sad and awful. The people whose lives are affected are real. I had been so enamored with that *People* cover of Claudine, all those photos of her and Andy walking into the courthouse—how beautiful, defiant, and glamorous she looked. Now the thing I think about the most is her kids being in the house that night she shot Spider. Then how she sent them all outside to wait for the ambulance. I picture them all crowded on the front porch in silence. Listening to the sirens get closer and closer.

I'm sure the reason I think about this is Thomas. That's the thing that *really* got the paparazzi going: him moving to L.A. with me. He needed a fresh start. There were photos of us all over Twitter. Then on every supermarket tabloid:

**A CHRISTMAS MIRACLE: ZARA SAVES LIVES
AND FINDS LOVE AT ASPEN SOIRÉE**

**THE COLORADO KID: THE TRAGIC TRUE
STORY OF ZARA'S NEW BEAU**

**LIAM WHO? THOMAS COOKE HELPS
ZARA GET HER GROOVE BACK**

Okay, I have to admit, I liked that last one.

So far things between Thomas and me are going great. I told him not to worry about finding a job for a while. I'm starting my tour in a few weeks, and he's coming with. In the meantime I suggested he take surfing lessons or some TM sessions. Try on California. He's doing those things but he can't stand not working, so he's tending bar a couple nights a week at a dive in Eagle Rock. Which is perfect. I don't want to say the name because I don't want anyone going there besides me and the regulars. I love it. Go in exhausted after my tour rehearsals. Just sit at the end of the bar with the locals. We small talk when things are slow. Nobody cares that I'm there. It's nice for a change. The only problem we're having is I think Pip likes him better than me.

As for the other Claudine, *my* Claudine, her trial was even quicker than Claudine Longet's. We briefly had to go back, both called as witnesses. They had it expedited so it was in mid-January. Aspen didn't need another high-profile murder on its hands and they wanted it over as soon as possible. This time I walked up the steps to the courthouse thinking about Thomas. I guess that's because he was holding my hand. His testimony was on day one and by day two Claudine had taken a plea deal. She'll be spending the rest of her life in prison but I think she gets nice sheets and like a window or something.

Calhoun + Calhoun was dissolved. I heard Jules now teaches yoga in Vail, and the other agents went to work for Steve.

Turns out, I did end up buying a house from him. Montague House. I had it torn down and gave the property to the Aspen Valley Land Trust on the condition they always keep it undeveloped. It was the right thing to do, especially since Thomas told me about the aspen trees. How they live and grow as communities. They have an interconnected root system and are technically the world's biggest living organism. They all need each other to survive. Now they'll have more room.

I also put up a plaque dedicating the land to Thomas's mom and dad. I wish I had gotten the chance to meet them. What a love story. The way she describes their romance in the letter—so epic. My favorite part is the postscript at the end, the way she tries to end it on a lighter note, let her son know that life is made up of all the little beautiful things, not just the huge overshadowing tragedies.

That seems right.

P.S. A few other important facts about your father: he couldn't care less about skiing, ate his steak rare and his hash browns burnt, loved avocado, ordered his eggs poached, dipped his french fries in mayo, drank his coffee black, liked long walks, never chewed gum, put hot sauce on his pineapple, made a killer grilled cheese, beat everyone he ever knew at horseshoes, played cards like a pro, was excellent at Scrabble, would take giant gasps when he laughed hard, and had a very small, uncharacteristic sneeze. He was perfect. Like you.